CRIME UPON CRIME

CRIME UPON CRIME

Michael Underwood

St. Martin's Press
New York

Library of Congress Cataloging in Publication Data

Underwood, Michael, 1916–
  Crime upon crime.

  I. Title.
PR6055.V3C7 1981   823'.914   80-51822
ISBN 0-312-17204-4

CRIME UPON CRIME

CHAPTER 1

'What's the name of the fellow who's just come in?'

'Arthur Kedby, do you mean?'

'The one wearing the pink tie.'

'That's Arthur Kedby.'

George Young, who knew every member of Noone's Club by name, lit a cigarette and gazed round the smoking room with a proprietorial air.

'What's he do?' his companion asked. 'I was talking to him in the bar the other evening and when we got on to the subject of jobs, I thought he became a bit evasive. I wondered if he belonged to one of those hush-hush outfits?'

'That'd be my guess, too,' George Young replied. 'In fact, he hinted as much to me on one occasion, since when I've always been careful not to embarrass the fellow by asking tactless questions. He doesn't come in to the club all that often. Probably spends a fair amount of time abroad on secret missions and that sort of thing. But he's quite a pleasant fellow.'

'He doesn't look much like a secret agent,' the other man replied, frowning at Arthur Kedby's pink tie, 'but perhaps that's all part of the game. I suppose you wouldn't get very far if everyone recognised you for what you were.'

'I once knew one of the top boys in M.I.5. Looked like

a village grocer. But he was obviously damned good at his job. Went off to Buck House to collect an honour when he retired.'

His companion grunted. 'Too many damned secret outfits if you ask me! Half the nation's on the government's payroll!'

It was George Young's turn to let out a grunt, as he hastily swallowed his drink and got up, murmuring something about having to see the secretary. Nobody could be more of a grinding bore than his companion on the subject of government expenditure and George Young knew from experience that prompt escape was essential.

Meanwhile, Arthur Kedby, who had particularly acute hearing, smiled to himself behind a newspaper as he settled back in one of the club's capacious leather chairs. It was not the first time he had overheard fellow members of Noone's speculating about what he did for a living. And should they ever find out the truth, he would certainly be asked to resign quietly or face expulsion. For Arthur Kedby earned his livelihood largely by crime.

Not spectacular crime, but crime of a sort that often went unreported to the police, if not actually undetected. The measure of his success was the fact that he had not only never seen the inside of prison, but had never even been charged with an offence. On the other hand, not for him the gigantic hauls of cash netted by those who meticulously planned bank hold-ups. His profits were as modest as the crimes he undertook.

But now as he sat in a corner of the smoking room of his club, hidden behind a newspaper, he sombrely contemplated his approaching fiftieth birthday. Sombrely, because he reckoned that once you reached your half-century, it behoved you to start thinking about providing for the sunset years of your life.

It was not that the sort of crimes he committed were physically exacting (for the most part they fell within the broad definition of cheating), but they required careful preparation and execution and it was entirely because he had always approached them in this manner that he had avoided trouble with the law. Nevertheless, they were mentally exhausting; moreover, just recently he had had a bad run, a lot of work with little reward. Sometimes he would spend weeks prospecting a promising seam, only to be thwarted at the end. Too late he would find out that he had been wasting his time and must turn elsewhere, which was always easier said than done. Victims had to be sought, they rarely presented themselves on a plate ready for plucking.

'Was it you who rang, sir?'

Arthur Kedby glanced over the top of his newspaper at the club servant who was hovering in front of him.

'No, not me, but as you're here, I'll have a large whisky and water,' he said with a quick smile.

Noone's Club was his one luxury in life. It not only provided him with respectability, but, more important, with a lot of high-level gossip which could sometimes be used to good account. Indeed, had he ever submitted a tax return, he could certainly have claimed his subscription as a business expense. It was a question of listening and observing and Arthur Kedby could be described as a professional in both capacities.

After all, it had been this trait which had led to his most profitable enterprise in recent years, namely the highly successful blackmail of a wealthy businessman, even if it had come to an abrupt end when his victim suddenly vanished and was never heard of again. Arthur Kedby had always suspected that he had taken himself off to Australia and settled there under an assumed name. He still experienced a touch of bitterness when he recalled the episode for, at the time, there had seemed to be no reason why the money should not go on coming in as regularly as a state pension.

9

He now reflected that, given the right circumstances, blackmail provided the best return of any crime. It was the nearest thing to drawing a pension and a nice pension was just what Arthur Kedby felt he needed as he approached his fiftieth birthday.

His drink arrived and he reluctantly reached for his wallet when the servant remained standing over him. Sometimes when they were busy and serving several people at once they would forget who had paid and who had not. It did not often happen, but it was always worth bearing in mind.

He folded the paper behind which he had taken refuge and placed it on the arm of the unoccupied chair next to him. Then he took a pleasurable sip of his drink and gazed about him. The smoking room was not more than a third full and though he knew most of the faces by sight, there was nobody who was more than a casual acquaintance. He was always polite and attentive when anyone spoke to him, but forming friendships was not his purpose in remaining a member of the club. He would have been hard put to say exactly what that purpose was. A subconscious yearning for respectability, perhaps; plus the contrast it afforded him with his otherwise somewhat seedy existence. For, in a world in which most people seemed to go up, Arthur Kedby had come down. From a sedate middle-class background, he had slid inexorably downwards until he had now reached the silty environment of Earls Court bed-sitterland. Not that he grumbled about this. After all, it was his chosen way of life and he had sufficient insight to recognise that it had been the defects of his own character that had led him on his gently downward path.

Two men had just come into the smoking room and he glanced towards them with casual interest. One was Philip Pym, a well known counsel, who was a member of Noone's; the other man was obviously his guest. Arthur Kedby was sure he had seen his face somewhere before.

Pym led his guest to a sofa against the farther wall and pressed the bell beside it.

'What'll you have to drink, Gerald?' he asked, as the smoking room waiter advanced towards them.

'I'll have a gin.'

'Gin and something or just gin?'

'Gin with a dash of water. A large one, if I may. I'm not sitting this afternoon, so can indulge myself,' Gerald said with a toothy grin.

It was at this moment that Arthur Kedby recalled why Gerald's face was familiar and, in so doing, experienced a sudden tingle of excitement, as well as a reminder of the hidden benefit of his membership of the club.

He thought it was a reasonable inference that Gerald was connected with the law. He and Philip Pym had the air of a couple of lawyers. Moreover, if he had heard right (and he had no doubt on that score), the reference to not sitting that afternoon seemed to imply that Gerald was a judge of some sort. And if Gerald was not only a judge, but also the man Arthur was sure he had seen ten days previously, an exciting new vista had suddenly opened up.

He watched their drinks arrive and noted Gerald's thirsty gulp of near neat gin. He felt like a spider quietly watching the complacent buzzing of a succulent-looking bluebottle. Not that there was anything particularly blue about Gerald's appearance. His face was red and strong-jawed and he had a thatch of light brown hair which was just starting to turn grey. Arthur decided that it was not the face of someone you would stop in the street to ask the way.

By the time he had finished his own drink, he was feeling far more cheerful and he even gave George Young's companion a friendly nod as he made his way out of the smoking room.

He walked across the hall to the glass-encased box where the porter sat.

'Do you happen to know the name of Mr Pym's guest?' he asked in a casual voice. 'I'm sure I recognise his face, but I can't think where I've met him.'

The porter glanced down at a list in front of him.

'He's a Judge Wenning, Mr Kedby.'

'Oh! Then I must be mistaken,' Arthur Kedby said with a self-deprecating smile. 'I don't think I've met anyone of that name.'

Feeling more cheerful than ever, he made his way along to the snack bar at the rear of the club.

One of Tony Ching's clients was just departing when Arthur Kedby arrived home.

Tony Ching and his friend Greg shared the basement flat and Arthur lived two floors above them in the same house which lay in a street off the Earls Court Road. It was a cosmopolitan district and in this particular street half the houses had been tarted up, while many others had flaking façades and dirt-encrusted windows. The house in which Arthur rented a one-room flat fell between the two extremes. People with skins of every hue and speaking every known tongue lived in the street, though most of the graffiti was currently Arabic.

Arthur had been about to open the main door of the house when he observed Tony Ching's visitor come up the steps from the basement and hurry away without a glance to left or right.

Tony and his friend Greg had only moved in a few months previously and it had not taken Arthur long to confirm his suspicion that, while Greg went off to some dreary office job each day, Tony Ching entertained male clients at the flat. At £20 a visit, as Arthur had subsequently found out by a simple ruse, involving an anonymous telephone call.

Though Tony's services held no interest for him, he had not lost an opportunity, since his discovery of what went on, of trying to catch a glimpse of visitors to the basement flat. In the meantime, he had established neighbourly contact with Tony Ching and made him aware of his knowledge, at the same time making it equally clear that he believed in live and let live.

After watching this latest visitor hurry off down the street, he made his own way down the narrow flight of steps that led to the basement area. It seemed a good moment to approach Tony. His visitors seldom followed each other in rapid succession at three o'clock of an afternoon.

The door opened a fraction and Arthur saw a pair of wary eyes peering at him. A second later, it was opened wide and Tony stood there with a beaming smile.

'Come in, Kedby. I make you some tea.'

'I'm not interrupting anything?' Arthur enquired delicately.

'I was just going out to the shops, but I can go later. So come in, Kedby!'

When they had first met and Arthur had introduced himself, Tony had said flatly that Kedby was a nicer name than Arthur and so Kedby he had become.

'How's Greg?' Arthur asked as he followed Tony towards the kitchen.

'He's always sulky. He doesn't like it that he has to go out. He quarrels with me when he comes home at night.'

'Does he mind your doing what you do?' Arthur had always been curious to know.

'Why should he? We have more money. He does not own me. Perhaps he should go back to his wife.'

'You mean Greg's married?' Arthur said in surprise.

'He has a baby. But he is confused. He doesn't know what he wants.' He turned his attention to the tea-making and handed Arthur a delicate porcelain cup. 'I think you like Chinese tea, Kedby?'

'It's very refreshing.'

'I go back to Hong Kong for holiday this year, so Greg will have to find another friend or go back to his wife,' he went on. 'My mother wants to see me again. I am her youngest. All my brothers and sisters are married.'

'Do they all live in Hong Kong?'

'One of my brothers is a policeman. Two of my sisters live in Australia.' With a serious expression he went on, 'But it is very expensive to fly to Hong Kong. That is why I must make much money.' With a small, sad shake of his head he added, 'Sometimes I get very tired.' He gave Arthur an indignant look. 'Why do you laugh at me, Kedby?'

'I'm not laughing at you, Tony; merely at the thought of your work being tiring.'

'But it is. And sometimes the people who come are not nice. Not nice at all. Of course it is better with regulars, but some of them do not respect me and I do not like that. Why should they not respect me?'

Arthur made a soothing noise and decided it was time to broach the object of his visit. Before he could speak, however, Tony went on, 'One of my regulars has just been for the last time. I am sad, but he is getting married again and it will be difficult for him to come.' He made a tiny moue with his lips. 'Many of my clients are married, but they like to try something different,' he added with a sly smile.

'Do you know somebody called Gerald, Tony?'

The Chinese boy's expression became wary. 'Why you want to know, Kedby?'

'He's a man in his fifties with a florid complexion and a lot of light brown hair turning grey.'

'Why you want to know, Kedby?' Tony repeated.

'He shows a lot of teeth when he opens his mouth. Do you know who I mean, Tony?'

'You have seen him come here?' Tony's tone was suspicious.

Arthur nodded. 'His name's Gerald, isn't it? I might be able to help with your fare home, Tony, if you answer my questions.'

'How much?'

'Ten pounds now and ten pounds later.'

It seemed from Tony's expression that he didn't regard the offer as especially munificent.

'What do you want to know, Kedby?'

'How often has Gerald visited you?'

'Three times. I do not like him. He has no respect. He is sadist, but I not allow him to do what he wants even for fifty pounds. He does not respect me and I do not respect him.'

'Do you know anything else about him, Tony? What his other name is or what he does for a living?'

'He said his name was Gerald. He did not tell me any more and I do not ask him questions.'

'No, of course not. But he never dropped a hint about his job?'

'No. I don't like him and don't want to know anything about him. I just take his money and give him massage. I would not care if he did not come back.'

'But he has,' Arthur observed thoughtfully. 'What was the interval between his visits?'

'Two weeks, maybe three. You like some more tea, Kedby?'

'Thanks. And here's the ten pounds I promised on account. I'll give you another ten later.'

'When?'

'When I have more myself.'

Tony put the folded ten-pound note under the teapot and gave Arthur a seraphic smile. A depraved little seraph, Arthur reflected as he lifted the dainty cup of aromatic tea to his lips.

A few minutes later Tony's phone started to ring and Arthur listened to him stating his tariff for the benefit of

15

another potential client. It seemed a good opportunity to slip away with a quick farewell wave.

It was only just after half past three and he decided to visit the public library, where it did not take him long to find the information he sought.

A search in two reference books told him all he wanted to know about Judge Gerald Wenning. That he was fifty-four and had been a judge for three years. That he was based at West Middlesex Crown Court and lived at Gerrards Cross. That he had a wife named Diana (*née* Fielding) and a daughter who had been born in 1955. And that his main (publicly admitted) recreation was shooting.

Well satisfied, Arthur Kedby returned home to plan his next move.

CHAPTER 2

At one point towards the end of an undistinguished career at a not very illustrious private boarding school, Arthur's form master had said in an exasperated outburst, 'I don't begin to understand you, Kedby. You show little enthusiasm for work and still less for games. Surely there's something you want to do in life?'

Arthur had given the indignant man a pacific smile before replying. 'I'd like to make money,' he had said after some thought.

'Are you being deliberately impudent?' the master had asked, suspiciously.

'No, sir.'

'How do you want to make it? Presumably you've given the matter your thought.'

'As easily as possible.'

'And what will you do with all this money you hope to make?' the master had enquired with scorn.

'Nothing special, sir. Just live.'

Later his form master had remarked to a colleague, 'He hasn't a spark of ambition and I doubt, moreover, whether he possesses a single moral scruple. I'd find him easier to understand if he were an out-and-out bad egg. At least one knows how to deal with a real villain, but Kedby doesn't

17

even have the determination to become that. Heaven knows where he'll finish up in life's great rat race.'

'If you ask me, he has all the makings of a minor crook,' the colleague had replied with the cynicism he invariably displayed when talking about schoolboys.

For no particular reason, Arthur was recalling this and other unsatisfactory encounters with his form master as he lay in bed that night. To him, school had been a barely supportable existence and his happiest day had been the one when he walked through its portals for the last time.

He had been the only son of elderly parents who had died within two years of each other when Arthur had been in his early twenties. The immediate effect had been to free him from the only sense of obligation he had ever felt. Although he and his father had remained strangers to one another up to the very end, he had been as fond of his mother as he could be of anyone and her death had left him anchorless. He mourned her passing, but was consoled by the ten thousand pounds she left him. The income it provided had not been sufficient to live on and hence he had been obliged to dip into capital or supplement it with extramural earnings whenever possible.

It was a combination of ever shrinking capital and his approaching fiftieth birthday that had caused Arthur to think a lot about his future in recent days.

But now, with luck, Judge Gerald Wenning was going to be able to help, albeit unwillingly.

Arthur did not own a car, but hired one when need arose. It was part of his plan to do so the next day and drive first to West Middlesex Crown Court which, he had discovered, was situated at Uxbridge, and then on to Gerrards Cross. Time spent in reconnaissance is seldom wasted, he had once read in a book of military memoirs. It had better not be, he reflected a trifle grimly as he switched off his bedside lamp. Especially not a reconnaissance involving the expense of a hired car. It was, however, a measure of his optimism that he had no hesitation in deciding to rent one for the occasion.

He set out at ten o'clock the next morning and drove down the A40 to Uxbridge, something considerably easier said than done at any hour of the day. Leaving the car in a public car park, he walked the two hundred yards to the Court, which was a new red-brick building.

There was a throng of people on the pavement outside the entrance and the vestibule had the air of the departure lounge of a fogbound airport. Everyone looked bored or resigned, but the smell of suppressed nervous apprehension was unmistakable.

Two courtrooms led off the vestibule and Arthur studied a list pinned inside a glass case which was stuck on the wall between their respective entrances.

Judge Wenning was sitting in court number two which was the one on the right. There was a reference to courts three and four which he assumed must be upstairs.

A uniformed policeman standing outside number two court gave Arthur a casual glance as he pushed his way through the swing doors. There was an unoccupied seat at the end of a bench just inside the second set of doors and he sat down under the minatory eye of a large lady usher.

Before he had even done so, however, he knew that the judge on the bench was the same man who had been lunching at Noone's the previous day. The face was unmistakable even though his thatch of light brown hair now lay hidden beneath a judicial wig.

Arthur sat back quietly, not wishing to draw undue attention to himself. He had no desire to linger, but realised that an immediate departure might arouse curiosity. He became aware that the judge was about to pass sentence on a youth standing in the dock to his right.

'You're an unprincipled young scalliwag,' Judge Wenning said, not without an underlying note of relish. 'You appear to have respect for neither person nor property and

I am quite unable to find anything in your favour. In these circumstances, I certainly don't propose to waste more words on you other than say that you will go to prison for three years.'

'Bollocks to you too!' the defendant shouted back before being hustled away by two prison officers.

Under cover of this diversion Arthur tiptoed out.

It was with a feeling of relief that he got back into the car and continued his westward journey. Though it had been satisfactory to have gained confirmation that Judge Gerald Wenning was, indeed, the right target, he had found his few minutes in court a distasteful interlude, the judge having given every indication of being a thoroughly unpleasant man. Admittedly, that meant he would have no cause to feel any pity for his victim, not that he ever did have such qualms. But he could now see why Tony Ching had spoken of his client Gerald with contempt.

Arthur liked to believe that he had always recognised the hypocrisy in his own nature (his cultivated appearance of respectability amongst the members of Noone's) and he could not help wondering whether Judge Wenning had similiar insight. Perhaps those who continually passed judgment on others grew a protective shell to enable them to do their job without inhibition.

It took him only fifteen minutes to reach Gerrards Cross, but rather longer to find the road in which the Wennings lived. He didn't wish to make enquiries which might be later recalled, but eventually he found a plan of the town in the window of an estate agent.

The road he sought was on the south side of the common in an area of large, expensive houses, surrounded by well kept gardens.

The Wennings' house turned out to lie one from the end of a leafy minor road, which sported a variety of architectural styles. Theirs was neo-Georgian, the one next to it mock Tudor and on the opposite side was a pink-washed fortress complete with crenellations.

He had parked the car on the grass verge of an adjoining road and was approaching on foot wearing a purposeful air and carrying a long manilla envelope in one hand which he glanced at from time to time as if to check his bearings. He also had a slim briefcase tucked beneath his arm to enhance the impression of someone on lawful business.

There was a double garage on one side of the Wennings' house and its doors were open to reveal a small car. The empty space beside was presumably for the judge's.

A red Porsche was parked in the drive outside the front door. The car and the house's Georgian façade might have been posing for some expensive sales catalogue and Arthur almost purred with anticipation, for such a property must be worth at least two hundred thousand pounds at current prices. Judge Wenning was certainly not going to be able to plead poverty when the time came. And if in due course he was obliged to sell up and move into a more modest house, that would be no great hardship. He mustn't expect someone who lived in an Earls Court bedsitter to have his withers wrung. Not, incidentally, that Arthur had any intention of revealing his own circumstances to his intended victim.

Running between their property and its mock Tudor neighbour was a narrow footpath with a wooden fence on the Wennings' side and a beech hedge on the other. As far as he could see, it led to a wood which lay at the back of both properties.

He decided to walk down it in order to view the Wennings' house from the rear. He wasn't sure what more there was to learn, but, as he was here, he might as well make a thorough job of his reconnaissance.

The wooden fence was too high for him to see over the top, but he could hear the murmur of voices coming from the other side. There was a small knot-hole and he put his eye to it as if it were a telescope. Sitting out on a paved terrace were a middle-aged woman, whom he assumed to be Mrs Wenning, a younger woman who could well be her daughter and a man in his late thirties who had a heavy black moustache and wore dark glasses. Arthur decided that he was probably the younger woman's husband and also the owner of the Porsche. If he was right in his deductions, he was looking at a family scene, from which only Judge Wenning was missing.

He had just started to retrace his steps to the road when a voice startled him.

'This isn't a public footpath, you know!'

At first he couldn't see anybody, but then he became aware of a woman's face peering at him through the beech hedge. Her hair and clothes were virtually the same colour as the copper hedge so that she was almost invisible.

'I'm sorry, I didn't know,' Arthur said in an abashed tone.

'There's a notice at the top saying so.'

'I must have missed it.'

'Who are you looking for, anyway?' the woman asked in an aggressive tone.

'I thought the path might be a short cut to the road which runs parallel to this one.'

'Well, it's not. It merely leads to the wood and that's private property, too. Belongs to the people who live on the opposite side of the road.'

'Thank you for telling me,' Arthur said contritely. 'I'll be on my way.'

The woman withdrew from the hedge and he noticed she had a pair of pruning clippers in her hand. She had obviously heard him and come across to investigate.

He reached his car without further incident and quickly drove off. Ten minutes later he pulled up outside a country pub and went in for a pie and half a pint of beer. His morning's work had given him both an appetite and a thirst and he could have done with a much larger drink, but he wasn't going to jeopardise his plans by running the risk of being breathalysed. He was likely to run into snags enough without that.

Now that he had completed his preliminary work, he was ready to take his first serious and irrevocable step. He felt like a hurdler who knew that it was time to remove his tracksuit and get ready for the race proper.

CHAPTER 3

Tony Ching was coming up the steps from the basement flat as Arthur arrived home.

'Hello, Kedby, how are you?'

'Well, thank you, Tony. And you?'

'I am tired. Sitting waiting for the phone to ring makes me depressed. But now I go to the shops.'

He was wearing a blue T-shirt with U.C.L.A. on the front and a pair of very tight jeans. In one hand was the leather pouch in which he always carried his money and from the other dangled an empty plastic shopping bag.

'You like me to shop for you, Kedby?' he said.

'No, thanks, Tony. I'll probably go out a bit later.'

Giving Arthur a jaunty wave of his bag, he set off down the street with a delicate swagger.

Back in his own flat Arthur got out a pencil and a pad of paper and began to draft his letter to Judge Wenning.

This is a simple blackmail demand, he began, and then stared thoughtfully at the sentence. He didn't believe in flowery euphemisms. It was much better to come to the point in straightforward language. After all, blackmail was blackmail however many words you used.

I require an immediate payment of £5000, he went on. *This is to be followed by monthly payments of £200 for an indefinite period. These amounts are well within your*

24

means and will ensure your continuance as a judge. If they are not met, your career will end abruptly and in a public scandal. Judges should be careful of the Chinese company they keep. Post the £5000 in used £20 notes to Mr John Smith, c/o Post Restante, Trafalgar Square Post Office, WC2. It must be there within seven days of receipt of this letter.

He read through what he had written and pursed his lips. He would like to make it shorter, but didn't see what he could cut. The first demand must inevitably be explicit.

It should be mentioned that he possessed an Australian passport in the name of John Smith which he had bought in a pub from someone who had undergone a sex-change operation and had no further use for it. It had seemed a good buy at the time and had proved so on a number of occasions for purposes of identification.

As he sat gazing at what he had written, he realised there was always the risk that his victim would dash off to the police. Nevertheless he reckoned he was on as safe ground as he could hope to find with Judge Wenning. Even if he did go to the police and was promised the usual anonymity, it would be the end of his career and he could hardly hope to avoid a public scandal.

It was Arthur's bet, however, that he wouldn't go near the police, for, if he did, not only would his career be blasted, but there would be no guarantee that his blackmailer could be traced and brought to trial. And if he didn't report it, he had no option but to pay for Arthur's silence.

He sucked the end of his pencil in a meditative fashion before adding two final sentences.

Our mutual interest will be served by silence on my part and prompt payment on yours. Further instructions will follow receipt of the first £5000.

Satisfied with what he had written, he started to make

a fair copy on a sheet of cheap lined paper, using a blue ballpoint pen.

He had long ago decided that typewriters could be traps for the unwary and that you couldn't beat a message in anonymously printed capitals. Afterwards, he would throw away the pen he had used and destroy the pad of paper, so that nothing could be traced back to him even in the unlikely event of the police finding their way to his doorstep.

He marked the self-adhesive envelope 'Strictly Private' and, after brief thought, addressed it to the judge at West Middlesex Crown Court. There was no point in disclosing that he knew where the judge lived. Having recently read in the paper of someone being found guilty in court on the evidence of a saliva test, he moistened the stamp with water.

He was on his way to post the letter when he ran into Tony Ching returning from his shopping expedition.

'You like me to post that for you, Kedby?' Tony enquired obligingly, looking towards the letter in Arthur's hand.

Taken unawares, Arthur shook his head in embarrassment and quickly slipped the letter into his pocket. He was sure Tony hadn't seen the front of the envelope, not that anything, apart from the name Gerald, would have had any meaning for him. Nevertheless, he was a bright youth who was quite capable of making smart deductions.

'I have to go to the post office, anyway, Tony, I need some more stamps.'

The truth was that Arthur had never had any intention of posting it in the same district in which he lived and, a few minutes after parting from Tony, was on a bus to the West End. He got off at Hyde Park Corner and posted it in the first box he saw.

As it bore a first-class stamp, it should arrive at its destination the next morning.

He had given his victim seven days in which to pay, and

he reckoned it would be prudent to wait a further week before going to the Trafalgar Square Post Office to claim his mail.

For the next two weeks, therefore, he had best try and think of other things. If he didn't, he could envisage the days passing with agonising slowness.

CHAPTER 4

It was almost a week before Arthur realised he had not
seen Greg for several days. He would often catch sight of
him as he left to go to work just before nine o'clock every
morning.

He was a short, thickset youth with tight blond curly
hair. He had a bustling walk and he invariably slammed
the iron gate at the top of the basement steps so that a
metallic echo reached up through the building.

Arthur wondered if he and Tony might not already have
broken up and Greg had returned to his wife. Their sort
of relationship seldom lasted very long, usually ending in
recrimination or just falling apart after the onset of mutual
boredom.

It was exactly one week after he had posted his letter
that the first dramatic event occurred. Arthur had just
started to prepare his supper when his outside bell was
rung. Persistently and with seeming urgency.

'Who is it?' he said into the intercom.

'It's Greg. I must see you, Arthur.'

Arthur pressed the buzzer that released the catch on
the main door and stood waiting at his own door until
Greg appeared on the stairs.

'What's happened?' he asked as Greg plunged past him
into the flat.

Arthur shut the door and turned to find Greg staring at him with a mixture of bewilderment and fear.

'Tony's dead,' he blurted out. 'I've just found him. I'm scared, Arthur. What am I going to do?'

'First of all sit down and I'll get you a drink. Then tell me exactly what's happened.'

Shocked though he was by the news, Arthur found himself steadied by looking after Greg's needs.

Greg took a gulp of the whisky Arthur handed him and let out a splutter. 'I'm sorry,' he mumbled, 'It's strong.'

'It's neat. Better for you,' Arthur remarked.

'I've been away for the past three days,' Greg went on after a cautious sip. He threw Arthur a quick glance. 'We had a bit of a row last Saturday night and I walked out. I came back this evening and there was Tony lying on the bed. He'd been strangled with a belt. It was still round his neck and his face looked ghastly. I touched his hand, but it was quite cold.'

'Was he dressed?' Arthur asked in a voice that had a tremble.

'He didn't have any clothes on, but an eiderdown had been thrown over his body. The curtains were pulled and the light was on. It meant that he had been entertaining,' Greg added primly.

'Have you called the police?'

Greg shook his head and gazed at Arthur with horror.

'They'll have to be notified some time and it's much better that you should call them now and tell them what you've told me.'

'But they'll suspect me. They'll try and get me to confess,' Greg wailed.

'All you have to do is stick to your story. There can't be any evidence against you, if you didn't do it.'

'But when they find out that Tony and I quarrelled, they'll jump to the conclusion that I killed him out of jealousy.'

'I agree you may have some uncomfortable questions to answer, but it's far better to face them now than run away. If you disappear, they'll search for you and then it'll be that much harder to persuade them you're innocent and you'll also have to explain why you ran away in the first place.'

'You're the only person who knows I've been back and you wouldn't tell, would you, Arthur? When Tony's body is discovered, they need never know I'd found it earlier. So why can't I just disappear for a time?' His tone was urgent and pleading.

But to Arthur the thought of Tony's body slowly mouldering two floors below was not an agreeable one. 'They'll look for you just the same,' he said.

'I'll tell them I last saw Tony on Saturday night.'

'And will you tell them that you walked out after a quarrel? Will you tell them that, Greg?' He could see Greg wavering. 'Believe me, it's much better to face things now. And there's another thing, are you sure nobody saw you come back here this evening?'

For a second, Greg looked pole-axed. 'Oh my God! I clean forgot, I bought some peaches from the shop on the corner and the old girl said she hadn't seen me for a few days.'

'That's that then! The police are bound to make house to house enquiries and the old lady will mention having seen you. I take it she knows you and Tony shared a flat?' Greg gave a forlorn nod. 'Incidentally, what have you done with the peaches?' Arthur enquired.

'They're on the kitchen table.' Greg looked suddenly wistful. 'I bought them specially for Tony. He loved peaches. They were a sort of peace offering.'

'I suggest you call the police now, Greg,' Arthur said gently. 'You can use my phone if you like.'

'Yes, I couldn't go back to the flat with Tony still lying there.' He got up to go across to the telephone, but

30

abruptly sat down again. 'Will you call them, Arthur? You speak to them.'

'It'll sound better if you do. You're the person who made the discovery. You can stay here until the police arrive and then I'll go down with you.'

While Arthur watched him, Greg dialled 999 and asked stammeringly for the police service. When he was connected, he spoke so rapidly that he was required to repeat most of what he had said. Fortunately the person at the other end of the line was clearly used to extracting details from distraught callers and soon Greg was answering simple, straightforward questions.

While they waited for the police to arrive, Arthur refilled Greg's glass and poured himself a drink which he tossed down like an unpleasant medicine.

'I knew this would happen to him one day,' Greg said miserably. 'All those kinky men who used to answer his advert. A lot of them were downright vicious.'

'I suppose it was an occupational hazard,' Arthur remarked. 'It can happen to either sex who goes in for that sort of thing. Don't misunderstand me, Greg, I liked Tony very much. He was a far nicer person than many with greater pretensions.'

But Greg had sunk into a gloomy reverie and wasn't listening, so Arthur turned to his own thoughts.

Did he really believe that Tony had been murdered by a sadistic client? Or was his untimely death a direct consequence of Arthur's blackmail letter?

If the first, it was a brutal coincidence. If the second, a horrifying and totally unforeseen development.

Either way he felt shattered.

CHAPTER 5

Detective Chief Inspector Neil Pennerly of B Division was one of the newer breed of Metropolitan Police officer. In appearance he might have been a television producer or from the world of advertising or anything else covered by the modishly descriptive term young executive.

He was thirty-three and happily married with two children, one of each sex, which added to the image of sound middle-class conformity. However, he lacked most of the traditional police prejudices. He was regarded with faint suspicion by his older colleagues and with cautious approval by those who worked under him. Cautious because even those who knew him best felt that he kept them at a slight distance.

Arthur became aware of this as the two men sat facing each other in his flat. His cool gaze with clear grey eyes lent him an air of clinical detachment.

Two police cars were parked in the street outside and a uniformed constable stood guard at the top of the basement steps. Inside Tony's flat, forensic and fingerprint experts roamed from room to room under the watchful eye of two of D.C.I. Pennerly's subordinates.

'When did you last see Tony Ching, Mr Kedby?'

'I've been trying to think. Certainly not today.'

'Yesterday?'

'I think it was the day before. He was just going down the steps to his flat as I was coming out of the front door.'

'What time was that?'

'About half past three.'

'Did you speak to him?'

'No. I only caught a glimpse of him and I'm pretty sure he didn't see me, otherwise he'd have waved or called out. Sometimes I've seen him twice in the same day and then several days might pass without my seeing him again. We usually only met in the street coming and going.'

'Did you never visit the flat?' Quickly, Pennerly added, 'Visit him as a neighbour, I mean?'

'Sometimes when we met, he'd invite me in for a cup of Chinese tea which he was rather proud of.'

'I take it you knew that he was a male prostitute?'

'Yes. One couldn't help being aware of certain comings and goings.'

D.C.I. Pennerly got up and walked across to the window and looked out.

'You had quite a good view of the comings and goings from here,' he remarked.

'Yes, but I assure you I didn't spend my time watching.'

'No, of course not. But did you happen to notice any of his callers yesterday?'

'Not that I remember. I should explain that the most I normally ever saw was a furtively retreating back.'

'But you'd have seen their faces if they happened to be arriving, wouldn't you?'

Arthur felt himself break out into a small sweat and quickly ran his hand across his forehead.

'Not really.' He gave Pennerly what he hoped was a disarming smile. 'They used not to waste any time before diving down the basement steps. There hasn't been one I could have recognised afterwards.'

Pennerly digested the information in thoughtful silence.

'You seem to be the only occupant of the building, Mr

Kedby, who was on neighbourly terms with Ching and his friend,' he remarked after a while.

Though not put as a question, it was clear he expected an answer.

'That's probably because I've lived here longer than the rest. Most of the tenants are foreigners who don't stay more than two or three months. The names on the bell panel outside the front door are always being altered.'

Pennerly gave a brief nod. 'Have you known Mr French as long as you've known Tony Ching?'

'Is that Greg?'

'You didn't know his name was French?' Pennerly said in a tone of mild surprise.

'No, I didn't. In fact I didn't know him at all well. He was at work all day.'

'Nevertheless, you were the person to whom he immediately turned,' Pennerly observed in his disconcerting manner.

'Yes, though I don't find that surprising.'

'I'm not suggesting it is, Mr Kedby. Anyway, when did you last see Greg before this evening?'

'It must have been at least three or four days ago. I'd often hear him leave for work in the morning. He always clanged the iron gate at the top of the steps.'

'So you hadn't seen him this week at all?'

'No.'

'Not since you last saw Tony Ching?'

'No.'

'When I say seen, I include heard.'

'Same answer.'

'He'd quarrelled with Ching.'

'So he told me.'

'Did that surprise you?'

'The fact that he told me or the fact that they'd quarrelled?'

'The second, Mr Kedby.'

34

'No it didn't, because Tony had hinted to me that their relationship was going through a rough patch. He said that Greg had become moody and unsettled.'

'One way and another, you seem to have been quite a confidant.'

'I've explained that.'

'Do you think Greg might have killed his friend?'

Arthur shook his head vigorously. 'I'm sure he didn't.'

'Why are you so sure?'

'He was very fond of him. He returned this evening to make it up. He even brought peaches as a peace offering. He'd hardly have done that and then killed him.'

'I'm not suggesting he killed him this evening. Indeed he couldn't have. The preliminary medical evidence is that Ching had been dead for between eighteen and twenty-four hours.'

Arthur shuddered. 'Poor boy! I mean, the thought of his lying there dead since last night.'

'A lot of bodies have to lie waiting to be found much longer than that.' Arthur shuddered again and Pennerly went on, 'But Greg could easily have crept back here last night and murdered his friend. Lovers' quarrel and all that.'

'Then why return this evening bearing peaches?'

'Murderers have done odder things than that. A compulsion to revisit the scene of the crime, etcetera!'

'I still can't believe it was Greg. And surely the manner in which Tony was strangled bears much of the hallmark of a sadistic killer.'

'I'm inclined to agree with you,' Pennerly said to Arthur's surprise. 'But we still have to check Greg's alibi.'

'Where is he now?'

'He's gone along to the station to help us further with our enquiries.' As he spoke his grey eyes fixed Arthur with a stare that defied him to comment. 'If he's told us the truth, it won't be long before we let him go.'

He glanced about the room as though making a quick silent inventory of its contents. Arthur watched him uneasily. Thank goodness he had disposed of all the materials he had used for his blackmail letter.

Pennerly's gaze came back to rest on Arthur's face. 'You didn't see or hear any callers arrive at the basement flat last night, Mr Kedby? Say between seven and midnight?'

'No. I drew the curtains early as it was such a dark evening and I had the television on until I went to bed about half past eleven.'

'And you heard no untoward sounds during that time?'

'None.'

'Pity! Because that's almost certainly when Ching was murdered.'

'I hope you catch the man.'

'So do I, Mr Kedby. I regard unsolved murders as a personal affront. I don't mind telling you, however, that this sort of case makes for tough going. Until you can establish some link between victim and murderer, it's like swimming around in circles.' He let out a sigh. 'My guess would be that Tony Ching had quite a few potential murderers amongst his callers.' He got up and shook free his right trouser leg. 'If you do recall anything about last night, Mr Kedby, please get in touch with me at once. You never know, something may suddenly come to you out of the blue which could help us. Meanwhile, we'll slog away.'

As soon as his visitor had left, Arthur got himself a stiff drink. The last three hours had been a nightmare and he needed to calm himself before trying to sort out his thoughts.

By the time he went to bed, the police cars and the constable outside had departed and the basement flat lay dark and silent.

He realised that the police might well return and make a further search, but he took comfort in the knowledge that nothing would be found which could point to Judge Wenning as having been one of Tony's visitors. There couldn't be anything as Tony didn't even know his name apart from Gerald.

In the meantime he was determined to go to the Trafalgar Square Post Office the very next day. His original intention of waiting an additional week had been overtaken by events.

'That's all there is addressed to John Smith,' the clerk said, holding out an airmail letter bearing a New York postmark.

Arthur glanced at the name of the sender and shook his head. 'No, that's not for me,' he said. 'I don't know anyone of that name.'

The clerk dropped the letter on the counter beside him and shrugged. 'Sorry, but that's all there is,' he said with a visible loss of interest in Arthur on the other side of the glass divide.

When Arthur emerged from the post office, the sun had come out, though it did nothing to warm his spirits. It was only eight days since he had posted his letter, but, even having due regard to the vagaries of the postal service, his instinct told him that he was not going to receive a reply.

Or was Tony's death his reply? It was something he must now urgently consider.

It was a reasonable assumption that Judge Wenning would have realised that Tony could not himself have composed such a letter, but he may have believed it to have been written by someone on his behalf. Someone who would share with him the proceeds of blackmail. And he had been sufficiently alarmed by the threat of exposure to strike back viciously and without delay.

Arthur paused on the edge of the pavement waiting for the light to turn green. But *did* he really believe it was the judge who had murdered Tony? Surely he would never have risked another visit to the flat after receiving the letter! Moreover, even a judge who had strayed from the narrow path of moral rectitude would think twice before resorting to murder. Illicit dalliance, if you could call it that, was one thing, but murder . . . it was inconceivable.

After further reflection Arthur decided he could also dismiss the possibility of Judge Wenning having employed others to do the deed for him. Judges simply did not mix with the right people, their ties with those they sent to prison being hardly conducive to any more fruitful form of association.

That said, he was left with two conclusions. The first that Tony had been killed by a stray sadistic psychopath and the second that Judge Wenning had decided to ignore his letter, even though he had not reported it to the police. Arthur's precautions had satisfied him as to that.

As to the second there was only one thing to do. Send him a further letter.

CHAPTER 6

Judge Gerald Wenning would never forget the shock of receiving Arthur's first letter.

He was used to getting abusive missives from disgruntled litigants and the like and had taken Arthur's to be one such. It was on his desk when he arrived at court on the morning after Arthur had posted it.

He slit open the envelope and assumed the disdainful expression that becomes part of a judge's equipment.

In the split second of realising that this was no ordinary malcontent's letter, the blood in his veins seemed to freeze. A moment later he was panting and his head swam. He sat back in his chair and tightly closed his eyes. When he opened them again, the letter was still where he had let it fall. He forced himself to pick it up and read it again.

By now the initial surge of shock was beginning to subside and he merely felt a terrible weakness in his limbs as if he had just come out of a high fever.

Desperately he sought to recall in every detail the three visits he had made to Tony. Earls Court was not an area in which he knew anyone, so who on earth could have recognised him? He was sure he had given Tony no clue as to his identity. Moreover, the Chinese boy had shown an utter lack of personal interest in him, apart from his

39

money. To the best of his belief he and Tony had been the only two people in the world aware of his visits.

He now read the letter a third time, seeking to give it cool legal appraisal.

In the first place, it could not have been written by Tony himself. It was too well expressed. That could only mean that the Chinese boy had an accomplice. They probably worked a blackmail racket together, the accomplice keeping out of sight but later shadowing the potential victim to ascertain who he was and where he lived.

Judge Wenning frowned. He recalled that in each of his visits he had approached by public transport, leaving his car in one of the West End's underground garages. Moreover, there had been nothing about his dress which could have given him away. He had worn slacks and a jacket with a roll-neck shirt.

Though he had been quite unaware of being followed, this must have happened. But even if he had been followed as far as the car park, how had the person managed to trace him after he had driven away?

The only possible explanation was that on his second or third visit, Tony's accomplice had left a car ready in the same car park. On the other hand, he had never phoned Tony more than an hour in advance, so how had the necessary preparations been made?

But what emerged all too obviously was that he had fallen victim to a dirty scheming racket.

He had been consorting with male prostitutes on and off over several years and this was the first time anything had gone amiss, despite all his usual precautions. He wondered how many other of Tony's clients had been blackmailed. Presumably he and his accomplice only selected those who were vulnerable to pressure.

He felt his anger rising. Even though he hadn't committed any prosecutable offence, he had laid himself wide open to blackmail as the writer of the letter so starkly reminded him.

£5000! To be followed by £200 a month! That was a laugh, he reflected bitterly, seeing that he was already in debt to twice that amount.

He glanced at the clock on his desk, a parting gift from members of his chambers on his appointment as a judge. It was almost time to robe for court. His head was splitting and he reached for the drawer in which he kept a packet of aspirin.

God, what a dilemma! What on earth was he going to do? It would probably still be possible to borrow £5000, but what about the £200 a month for an indefinite period. He might be paying someone a pension for life. Little did he know at that moment how closely he was reflecting Arthur's hopes!

It seemed there were three courses open to him. To go to the police, to pay up or to ignore the letter and sit tight.

The first possibility was unthinkable and the very suggestion of it made him start to tremble uncontrollably. He watched his hands shaking with a mixture of dismay and revulsion.

To pay up was almost as unattractive a prospect.

On the other hand, to ignore the letter held various short-term advantages. Perhaps the letter was a bold try-on and if he ignored it, the writer would realise he had picked the wrong victim. In those circumstances, he would surely hesitate to repeat his blackmail. Accordingly, procrastination provided a glimmer of hope, where the other two options offered none.

Later he was to wonder how he ever got through that day in court. To the counsel appearing before him, he merely seemed more irritable than usual.

'You look worn out, dear,' his wife said when he arrived home soon after half past four that afternoon.

'I've had a vile day and I've got a splitting headache,'

41

he replied sourly. 'I'd like a cup of tea.'

'Why don't you go and lie down for a bit?'

'I will after you've brought me a cup of tea.'

'Christine and Douglas aren't coming till seven.'

'Oh God! I'd forgotten they were coming to supper.'

The last thing he felt like was the company of his daughter and son-in-law. It was always the same. As soon as supper was over, Christine and her mother disappeared into the kitchen, leaving him and his son-in-law to male talk, which usually meant Gerald Wenning relating a recent case in which he had emulated the wisdom of Solomon or packed some deserving crook off to prison and his son-in-law holding forth on a successful coup he had brought off in the antique world.

He and Christine ran a shop in a village on the edge of the Cotswolds where they appeared to conduct a flourishing business with a heavy emphasis on lucrative exports to Germany, Japan and South America.

There had been a time when Douglas Orden had stood in slight awe of his father-in-law, but it had long since passed. Nowadays he was apt to be patronising.

Judge Wenning drank his cup of tea in a morbid silence. His wife accepted that he had had a bad day in court which had given him a headache and decided that, like a bear with a sore head, he was best left alone.

She believed that he drank too much and that his liver lay at the root of most of his problems. But whenever she brought the subject up, he scowled angrily and became the hectoring, sarcastic lawyer. He had never taken kindly to criticism.

As he lay on his bed, curtains drawn to blot out the rest of the day, his mind worked feverishly to find some way out of his trouble. But the effect was that of rubbing a raw patch of skin.

He felt a trifle better after two strong drinks before dinner and he drank a lot more during the meal. Mother and daughter exchanged resigned glances and it was with a certain relief that they retired to do the washing-up, leaving Douglas to cope with his father-in-law.

'Did you discover what Daddy had on his mind?' Christine asked her husband later that evening as they drove home.

Douglas Orden shot her a quick glance in the darkness of the car. 'I wasn't aware he had anything on his mind.'

'It was obvious that he had. Mummy said he arrived home with a crushing headache and was particularly unforthcoming.'

'There's nothing new about that. He frequently has moody days when your mother can hardly get a word out of him. You've often told me so.'

'I know, but Mummy felt tonight was different. He looked awful and he was obviously drinking too much.'

'If I may say so, darling, there's nothing very new about that either.'

'Mummy believes that drink is the root cause of his moody behaviour.'

'Cause and effect,' he said in a musing voice. 'Often difficult to tell which is which.'

'You're hedging,' she said a trifle crossly. 'Is it money again? Is that what's troubling him?'

She knew that her father had borrowed money from his son-in-law and they had both agreed that this should be kept from her mother.

He let out a heavy sigh. 'Yes, I'm afraid it is,' he replied.

'Why couldn't you say so when I first asked?'

'I didn't want to worry you.'

Christine allowed this to pass without comment. 'Has he asked you for another loan?'

'Yes.'

'How much this time?'

'Five thousand pounds.'

She pondered this in silence before saying, 'I think he ought to see a psychiatrist. About his compulsive gambling, I mean. How much longer can he go on losing money like this? It's become an absolute nightmare. His career's in danger. The Lord Chancellor expects judges to lead lives which are beyond public reproach. The powers-that-be would be appalled if they knew about his gambling debts. He might even be asked to resign from the bench. Did he tell you how he'd come to lose such a huge sum?'

Douglas shook his head. 'He merely said it was the damned horses again.'

'It only needs some bookmaker to turn nasty and he'll be in terrible trouble.'

Her husband let out a mirthless laugh. 'The bookmakers won't turn nasty as long as he goes on paying.'

'As long as you go on paying them, you mean.'

'Same thing.'

'It'd kill Mummy if she ever found out.'

'It's remarkable that she's never guessed. She knows he bets heavily on the horses.'

'She thinks he breaks even over the year. That's what he's always told her.'

'I suppose she doesn't know that we now hold a mortgage on the house?'

'No, and she mustn't. I'm still unhappy about that, Douglas. Was it absolutely necessary?'

'I'm afraid I'm not prepared to lend money to anyone, even your father, without some form of security. It's normal business prudence.'

'But this was a family affair, not a business transaction.'

'I'm sorry, darling, but I had to think of our interests as well. We had to protect ourselves or, if the worst should ever come to the worst, we could be up the creek with your father.'

'Don't say things like that. It gives me the shivers.'

'I'm only facing reality.'

'Poor Mummy! I dread to think what would happen to her.'

'We'd help somehow,' he said, though without great enthusiasm.

'By the way, are you going to lend him the further amount?'

'I said I'd let him know.'

Christine gave an anxious squeal. 'When does he need it by?'

'He has a week to find it.'

'It's a never-ending nightmare,' she repeated. 'And what'll happen when we can't afford to lend him any more?'

'You know what gamblers are. He doesn't think that far ahead. Their luck is always about to change. Everything's going to be all right from now on, etcetera. Even an educated man like your father is capable of kidding himself.'

'I wonder if he really does.'

'As long as there's someone ready to bale him out, I doubt whether he'll alter.'

'That's a terrible statement.'

'Nevertheless, it's true. What's more, you know it, darling.'

'When are you going to let him know about the money?' she said after a pause.

'I said I'd call him in a couple of days.'

'But you are going to lend it to him, aren't you, Douglas? You must.' Her tone was urgent and imperative.

'Have I ever failed you?'

'No, but ...'

'Then stop worrying. Anyway, there are always other possibilities.'

'Other possibilities?' she said, frowning in the dark. 'What do you mean?'

'I'm probably in a better position to raise money than he is.'

'From the bank?'

'Banks are not the only people who lend money.'

'What do you have in mind?' she asked relentlessly.

'Let's talk about something else, shall we?' he said abruptly. 'You know you can rely on me, so let's leave it at that!'

Christine knew better than press him further, though his words did little to allay her anxiety. She was aware that he had various business contacts of whom he spoke brusquely and with unwillingness. That side of the business, as well as its finance, was entirely his and she never interfered. Her only part was to serve in the shop. From time to time there were deals which he was reluctant to discuss and she accepted the situation, though she could not help noticing that they invariably involved the same people. Two brothers, Ron and Percy Sugarman, who appeared to be a couple of cheerful extroverts, but whose presence always made her feel uncomfortable.

Douglas had told her that they traded in various street markets, but, in his view, knew more about most aspects of the antique business than a lot of dealers with high-class shops.

On their visits to the Orden shop, they usually arrived in a gleaming new estate car, though, occasionally, by contrast, in a dilapidated transit van.

The last half-hour of their drive home was accomplished in silence.

It was as they were getting out of the car in the garage that Douglas said, 'I've just remembered I've got a phone call to make. But you go on up to bed.'

'A phone call at this hour?' she said. It was just on midnight.

'It won't take long.'

'But who on earth are you going to call?'

She could tell from his expression that he resented being questioned. His features seemed to assume an additional heaviness and he glowered at the night sky.

46

'Percy Sugarman, if you must know. I promised to phone him tonight. He always watches television until close down, so he won't be in bed. Now are you satisfied?'

As she made her way upstairs, she heard him close his study door. She hoped that the telephone call to Percy Sugarman coming so soon after her father's request for more money was mere coincidence.

Admittedly, Douglas had implied that it was the fulfilment of an earlier promise, but she still felt uneasy.

On the other hand, she reflected bleakly, wouldn't a loan from the Sugarmans be better than have her father face otherwise certain ruin?

When her husband did come upstairs to bed he undressed in silence, save for some tuneless humming beneath his breath. A sure sign that he was not in a mood to talk. She was all the more surprised, therefore, when he got into bed beside her and immediately began making love.

'Let's forget your father and his troubles just for a few minutes, shall we?' he said with a lecherous smile.

In the event, Christine found herself only too ready to fall in with his suggestion.

CHAPTER 7

Arthur had been minded to refer to Tony's death when he sat down to draft his second letter, with a view to extracting an additional premium out of His Honour Judge Gerald Wenning.

After reflection, however, he decided to resist the temptation to throw down the gauntlet quite so crudely. It would be a different matter if he had definite proof of the judge's complicity in Tony's murder, but if, in fact, he had had nothing at all to do with it, he, Arthur, would have weakened his hold by making such a wildly false assumption.

So thinking, he tore up the piece of paper on which he had been writing and began again. He was determined to make this letter short and to the point.

You ignored my first letter so this is your last chance. Post £5000 in used £20 notes to Mr John Smith, c/o Post Restante, G.P.O. Howick Place, SW1 to arrive by next Wednesday or face the consequences of disclosure of your visits to our late Chinese friend, of which there is still proof.

He decided to say *late* Chinese friend to indicate that he was aware of Tony's death and wasn't repeating his demand in ignorance of it, a fact the judge might misinterpret. He also added the final six words in case Wenning should believe that all evidence had disappeared with Tony's death. He then underlined them to add a touch of menacing emphasis.

The use of a different Post Restante address was a further precaution, though he had selected another large and busy office.

After he had addressed and sealed the envelope and stuck on a first-class stamp, he destroyed the materials he had used. This seemed more than ever desirable as he was by no means sure he had seen the last of Detective Chief Inspector Pennerly with his cool, appraising look and large grey eyes which at times seemed to have X-ray properties.

It was a second later that he had a stroke of inspiration. It came as he was wondering where to post the letter. In Gerrards Cross, of course. That would give Judge Wenning something to think about when he saw the postmark, leading him to assume that his blackmailer was a local person. So be it, Arthur reflected with satisfaction.

It was only midday and if he set out now, he could be back in London again by late afternoon. It wasn't worth hiring a car merely to go and post a letter, so he would have to make the journey by train.

As he descended the porch steps, he saw Greg coming along the street. He had not spoken to him since the evening he sought refuge with Arthur after discovering Tony's body, though he thought he had seen a light in the basement the previous day and had wondered if Greg might have returned.

'Hello, Greg,' he called out in a friendly voice as Greg approached, head down and eyes fixed on the pavement.

'Oh hello,' Greg said, looking up.

'Are you living back here again?'

'I came back yesterday. The police said they didn't mind. But I don't know how long I'll be staying.' He gave a helpless shrug. 'I've thrown up my job and I've no idea what I'll be doing.'

'Have you heard how the police are getting on with their enquiries?' Arthur asked.

'Once they had to let me go, I suspect they lost hope.'

'I'm delighted you were able to satisfy them so quickly, Greg.'

'Not as much as I am! They really grilled me. Nothing physical, mind you, but the same questions over and over again. I suppose they hoped I'd trip up.'

'Have they any clues?'

'I imagine they're working their way through all the addresses and telephone numbers in Tony's book.'

'Whose numbers would they be?'

'A few of his regulars, but mostly boys he'd met in pubs and clubs and had one night stands with.' Greg let out a harsh laugh. 'Tony was born promiscuous. He couldn't help himself. It was one of the things we used to quarrel about.'

'And the police think it may have been one of them who murdered him?'

'Why not? It probably was. Not that they'll be able to trace a lot of them. They're not people with fixed addresses.'

'Used Tony to mix much with other Chinese?'

'That was another thing we quarrelled about. He'd go off to one of their clubs on a Saturday night and not come home for twenty-four hours.'

'What'd he be doing all that time?'

'Talking and drinking and gambling. The Chinese love gambling.'

'I probably shouldn't ask this, Greg, but was Tony into drugs at all?'

'Not in the sense you mean. He didn't go in for any of the hard stuff. He might take a puff of a joint at a party, but that was all.'

'Have you told the police all this?'

'They seemed to know most of it anyway.' He gave

Arthur a thin smile. 'They wanted to know about you.'

'Me!' Arthur felt a sudden stab of panic. 'What did they want to know about me?' he asked in an anxious voice.

'What your relationship was with Tony and things like that.'

'I hope you told them it was a purely neighbourly one.'

'Yes.'

'And did they seem satisfied?'

'You never really know what the police are thinking, do you?' Greg said unsatisfactorily.

'Well, what other questions did they ask about me?'

Greg shuffled uncomfortably. 'What did I know about your home life and things like that. Were you married and, if so, what happened to your wife? Did I think you were gay? You know the sort of thing.'

'And what did you tell them?' Arthur asked in a bleak tone.

'I told them I didn't know. Well, I don't, do I?' he burst out under Arthur's stern stare. 'I don't know any more about you than you do about me. We've just been good neighbours like you said.'

'*I* told the police I was sure you hadn't murdered Tony,' Arthur said in a tone of sad reproof.

'Thanks.' Greg looked discomfited, as well he might in Arthur's opinion. It was all too clear that, even if he hadn't actually landed Arthur in the muck, he had not gone out of his way to convince the police what an impeccable fellow he was.

Standing there on the pavement, Arthur could almost feel his letter to Judge Wenning scorching the inside of his pocket with its guilty secret.

'Well, I must be getting on,' he said coolly, and made to walk away.

'Let's have a drink one evening,' Greg said, as if seeking

to make amends. 'I probably shan't be here much longer and I'd like to say goodbye before I leave.'

'Give me a call and we'll try and fix something,' Arthur replied in the same coolish tone.

His encounter with Greg had had an unsettling effect on him and it wasn't until his train to Gerrards Cross had broken through the outer barrier of built-up London and was trundling through green countryside that his spirits lifted.

The first thing he did on arrival was to check the trains back to London. There was one in fifteen minutes' time which would enable him to accomplish his mission and return on it.

As he emerged from the station, he noticed a couple of boys observing him. One spoke to the other who giggled. They were about ten years old and, like most grown-ups, Arthur found it inhibiting being laughed at by children without being aware of the cause. He affected not to see their amusement, but took an early opportunity of studying his reflection in a shop window to ascertain if there was any obvious reason for their mirth. He could find none.

He walked to the post office which was no distance and with a seemingly nonchalant air popped his letter into the box.

On retracing his steps to the station, he once more noticed the two boys, who were now on the opposite side of the road apparently engrossed by a shop-window display.

Ten minutes later he was on his way back to London. As he gazed out of the train window a tiny niggle of doubt crept into his mind. Unless the post went haywire, his letter must reach West Middlesex Crown Court the next morning, but that would be Friday, and supposing Judge Wenning only worked a four-day week or was despatched to sit at a different court? He believed this sometimes happened. In either event his letter might not be received for several days.

There was nothing he could now do about it, however, except hope. Nevertheless it made him reflect once more that chance was always lurking just out of sight waiting to upset the best-laid plans.

In this instance, chance stayed her hand and Arthur's worries had been needless, for not only did the letter arrive on time, but Judge Wenning arrived at court a few minutes after it had been put on his desk with other mail.

He recognised it as soon as he picked it up and let it fall from his fingers as though it were singeing them. The carefully printed words on the envelope were unforgettable and then with sudden shock he noticed the postmark.

It was a minute or two before he could bring himself to open it and read the contents. In one sense, they came almost as an anti-climax.

After a slight pause, he thrust the letter into his jacket pocket as if it were an outstanding bill about which something would have to be done. Then noticing the envelope still on his desk, he picked it up and stuffed it into the same pocket.

CHAPTER 8

On the morning that the second letter was delivered, Christine decided to telephone her mother. She and Douglas drove over to have supper with her parents about twice a month, but had not been since the occasion of her father's request for the further loan. Sunday lunch was the time for the return hospitality but, for one reason and another, the older couple had not paid a visit for several weeks. When these gaps in visiting occurred, Christine always made a point of calling her mother.

She had become increasingly worried about her father's money troubles and where it would all end, her concern being chiefly for her mother who apparently had no inkling of the sums her husband had borrowed from his son-in-law.

A few days after their last visit to Gerrards Cross, Christine had asked Douglas to confirm that he would be lending her father the further £5000. He told her that he had, as promised, spoken to him on the telephone, but that the urgency for the loan had evaporated and everything was all right for the time being.

Good news as this was from their personal financial point of view, it had failed to quench her anxiety. She assumed that some creditor had lifted the pressure; but for how long? It sounded no better than a piece of temporising somewhere along the line.

When she asked her husband for further details, he said he didn't know any more and urged her to stop worrying.

He hinted that he regretted having ever told her of her father's problems in the first place.

'It was stupid of me,' he had said.

'No, it wasn't, Douglas. I had to know. But it's only natural that I worry.'

'Well, stop doing so because we'll see him through somehow.'

Douglas was in the converted barn which served as a warehouse when she went up to their bedroom to make her call. As she dialled her parents' number, she reflected how much closer she had come to her mother in recent years. When she was growing up she had adored her father, but slowly her feelings had swung round as she was made more and more aware of his feet of clay.

Since her marriage three years earlier at the age of twenty-two, the bond between mother and daughter had strengthened. Though she was still fond of her father, it was more for what he had been than for what he was.

One of the turning points had come when, shortly after his appointment as a judge, he had invited her to accompany him to court and hear him try a case. She had come away shocked by his behaviour, which had been rude and overbearing to all and sundry. It mattered not that he was probably right in his rulings and that one of the defending counsel was singularly inept and a number of witnesses remarkably obtuse, nobody, she felt, should exercise their authority in such a despotic fashion.

It had been a traumatic occasion which she had never forgotten and though there had been subsequent invitations to see him on the bench, she had always made excuses.

It was ironic, too, she reflected while now waiting for her mother to answer the phone, that her father had actually raised objections to her marrying Douglas on the grounds of their age difference and that he didn't have what he referred to as a proper job.

'There may not be all that difference between forty and fifty or fifty and sixty,' he had said, 'but between twenty-two and thirty-two it's the difference between worldly innocence and mature experience. Also, this dabbling in antiques isn't really a job.'

Christine wondered whether he ever recalled any of this when approaching his son-in-law for money.

Her thoughts were interrupted by her mother's voice on the line.

'Sorry I've not phoned before, Mummy, but life has been rather hectic the last few days. Douglas has been away at sales and Mrs Parkes, the woman who helps out in the shop, chose that moment to fall off her bicycle and bruise her leg. But she's now back. Anyway, how are you?'

'I seem to spend my time sweeping up leaves in the garden. It's the one time of year I wish we didn't have so many trees around us.'

'Can't the old boy do them?'

'He only comes one afternoon a week and I'm not paying him two pounds fifty an hour to sweep up leaves.'

'How's Daddy?'

'He seems better.'

'Oh good!' Christine said with a feeling of genuine relief. 'I expect he had a virus of some sort.'

'It'd be nice to think so, but I've never hidden from you what I believe to be the cause of all his ailments. If only he wouldn't drink so much!'

'I was saying to Douglas on the way home the other evening that I wished he'd see a psychiatrist. Is there any chance?'

'None. He won't even admit he has a drink problem

and, as every cure depends on the patient's co-operation, it's a hopeless situation from the very start.'

'At least he has a long way to go before he's a true alcoholic.'

'I don't know what the yardstick is,' her mother said with a sigh. 'As far as I know it's not yet affecting his work, which is a mercy.'

There was a pause and then Christine said, 'Why don't you both come to lunch on Sunday? I know it's rather short notice, but, unless you're doing anything else, we'd love to see you.'

'We were to have gone to the Pyms' that day – you know, Philip Pym is head of Daddy's old chambers – they've just moved to somewhere near Basingstoke – but Hazel Pym has been rushed into hospital for an emergency operation.'

'Then come here instead.'

'I'd better just confirm it with Daddy when he comes home this evening, though I don't expect he's fixed up anything else.'

'Call me tonight and let me know.'

'I've just remembered, he's going to a dinner in town and has taken his evening wear with him so that he needn't come back here to change. May I let you know in the morning?'

'That'll do fine.'

'I'll probably be in bed and asleep by the time he returns. It's one of those "no wives" dinners and they always last much longer.'

'I don't let Douglas off the leash to attend those sort of functions,' Christine said with a small laugh.

The truth was that the occasion had never arisen and she was fairly sure that, if it did, she would be presented with a *fait accompli*. She had always chosen, however, to pretend to her parents that she and Douglas were equal partners in their marriage and neither did anything without consultation with the other. Like other aspects of living, this was the truth in a limited form.

After she had rung off she went downstairs to meet Douglas coming in from the warehouse.

'Been shifting things round a bit,' he observed. 'Percy Sugarman's delivering some furniture later this morning.'

Christine was in the shop when the van drew up outside.

'And how's my favourite girl?' Percy exclaimed as he gave her a smacking kiss on the cheek. 'Is the lord and master around?'

'He's in the warehouse,' Christine said, recoiling from the familiar smell of stale cigar and after-shave lotion which Percy Sugarman always exuded.

'Right, I'll back the van down and we'll get it unloaded.'

'What have you brought?'

'A Welsh dresser and a chest of drawers. Won't take long.'

A few minutes later when she went into the office at the rear she watched them manoeuvring the two items out of the van. The Welsh dresser was obviously a beauty, but the chest of drawers was bad Victorian and hideous. She wondered what had induced Douglas to buy it and concluded that it must have been part of the deal involving the dresser.

She went into the kitchen to make coffee, but it was half an hour before her husband and Percy emerged from the warehouse.

'I was beginning to think you must have got locked in,' she remarked when they eventually appeared.

'Why was that, sweetheart?' Percy enquired with a faint frown.

'You were in there so long.'

'Ah! That was my fault. I was nattering on to Doug about my Jeanie. Comes top in everything. Her teachers say she's the brightest kid they've ever known. Well, I

58

must be on my way back as soon as I've drunk a lovely cup of coffee.'

Later when she and Douglas were eating their customary frugal lunch she said, 'Have you ever met Jeanie?'

'Jeanie who?' he asked.

It made her wonder what they really had been talking about all that time.

'What made you buy that ghastly chest of drawers?' she enquired during one of the silences that punctuated their meal.

'Because I know where I can sell it,' he said a trifle petulantly.

'Oh! I thought it might be part of a package deal with the dresser.'

'In a way, yes.'

'Who's going to buy it?'

'Cannons.'

Cannons were noted for purchasing the complete contents of houses at bargain prices, selling off what they could at a handsome profit and converting what was left into firewood. That, at any rate, was the popular belief in the locality.

There was something in Douglas's manner that prevented her asking further questions and the matter was, anyway, shortly to be driven clean out of her mind.

It was just after seven o'clock the next morning that they were awakened by their bedside phone.

It was her mother, not calling to say whether they would be coming to lunch on Sunday, but to break the news, in a voice distorted by emotion, of her father's death.

CHAPTER 9

Diana Wenning had half-woken twice during the night and been aware that her husband's side of the bed was still empty.

She knew that sometimes when he returned home late from a function he slept on the divan bed in his dressing room which was kept made up for such an eventuality.

When her alarm woke her at seven o'clock and she found that she still had their bed to herself, she got up and went along to the dressing room to make sure he was there. But it was empty and its bed lay undisturbed.

For a moment she stood perplexed and mildly apprehensive. She prayed that he had not been involved in an accident on his way home, or, worse still, been stopped by the police and breathalysed. It was something she had long dreaded.

On the other hand, if he had not felt fit to drive home, perhaps he had stopped the night in town. He always had the offer of several beds with friends.

On her way back to their bedroom, she paused to look out of the landing window which faced toward the front. By craning her neck, she saw that the garage doors, which she would have expected to find open if he had not come home, were in fact closed.

Putting on her dressing-gown she hurried downstairs.

Perhaps he was asleep on a chair in his study. There was no sign of him, however, in any of the rooms.

With mounting anxiety, she let herself out of the house and hurried round to the garage, shivering in the first light of a grey morning. She might have guessed that the doors would be locked, so that she had to return to the house for the key.

At last she got them open, only to confirm her worst fears. Her glance fell immediately on a length of hose-pipe which snaked its way from the exhaust pipe into the interior of the car via a rear window which clamped it in position. Several pieces of rag sealed the gap on either side of the pipe.

Her husband lay in a foetal position on the rear seat with a blanket covering his body apart from his head.

With a small cry of horror, she tried to wrench open the door, but it was locked, as she quickly discovered the others to be as well.

The ignition light was glowing dimly and she realised that the engine had gone on running until there was no petrol left in the tank.

She rapped frantically on the window nearest her husband's head, but knew it to be a futile gesture.

She dashed back into the house for his spare car keys, returning to confirm the harsh truth: that he was quite dead and beyond any resuscitation.

It was at this juncture that she returned indoors and telephoned her daughter.

'I'll get dressed and come straight away,' Christine said with commendable practicality, after expressing her shock. 'I'll be with you in about an hour and a half.' She glanced at her husband who appeared to have turned over and gone to sleep again. 'We'll both come. Mrs Parkes can look after the shop.'

'Wake up, Douglas,' she said as she replaced the receiver. 'Something terrible has happened.'

61

'What d'you say?' he asked sleepily.

'Daddy's dead. Mummy found him sitting in the car in the garage. He'd been asphyxiated by exhaust fumes. We must go over immediately.'

'Oh, my God!' he said in a tone in which Christine thought she discerned a note of consternation blended with his surprise. 'Do you mean he's killed himself?'

'Yes.'

Diana Wenning had, meanwhile, called the police. She asked to speak to Inspector Morrow whom she had met on several occasions and who appeared to have responsibility for the safety of V.I.P.s living in the district. As a judge, Gerald Wenning qualified for special attention from the police. For example, Inspector Morrow had advised them on security locks and other burglarproof devices and, on one occasion, had called after the judge had received a threatening letter at his home. The writer later turned out to have been recently released from a mental hospital to which Judge Wenning had committed him.

After asking one or two practical questions, Inspector Morrow had said in a reassuring voice, 'Don't touch anything, Mrs Wenning, and I'll be over very soon.'

She was waiting by the open front door when their car turned into the drive. Inspector Morrow jumped out first, followed by a younger man whom he introduced as Detective Sergeant Allen and a slip of a girl who was Woman Police Constable Stokes.

'You take Mrs Wenning back into the house, Sally,' he said to the woman P.C., 'and look after her while Sergeant Allen and I have a look in the garage.'

When, about fifteen minutes later, the two men came in, W.P.C. Stokes and Diana Wenning were drinking tea in the breakfast alcove adjoining the kitchen.

Diana hadn't particularly wanted any tea, but felt it was expected of her. It also gave W.P.C. Stokes something to do. With the arrival of the men she was required to repeat her story of what had happened.

'Had he ever mentioned suicide, Mrs Wenning?' Inspector Morrow asked.

'Never.'

'Did he have any worries as far as you know?'

'No, though he was inclined to be rather moody at times.'

'What brought on the moods?'

'I'm afraid he sometimes drank rather heavily. In the evenings, that is. He was always perfectly fit for work the next day.'

Detective Sergeant Allen wrinkled his nose. He was a blond-headed young man of tough physique who had appeared in front of Judge Wenning on two occasions. The judge's reputation as a drinker was more widely known among the police than his wife would have cared to believe.

Inspector Morrow nodded gravely. 'We'll be able to find out from the people he was with at dinner last night what sort of mood he was in when he left to drive home. They'll be able to fill us in on all those details.' He was a comfortable-looking man with a comforting sort of voice and had always been good at putting people at their ease. If he had not been a police officer, he'd have made an excellent undertaker, as his less charitable colleagues were apt to aver.

'Have you looked to see if he left a note of any kind, Mrs Wenning?' Sergeant Allen asked in the pause that followed.

'Where would he have left it?' she asked vaguely. 'I didn't look inside the car.'

'There's nothing in the car. I just wondered if he might have let himself into the house and left one on the hall table or . . .' He glanced about him. '. . . well, really anywhere.'

The others allowed their gazes to roam around the room

as though they were playing a party game.

'Has the postman been yet, Mrs Wenning?' Sergeant Allen asked suddenly.

'I haven't heard him. I've not looked . . .' She broke off and gave a small exclamation. 'Oh, you don't think . . .'

'I'll go and see if there's anything in the box on the door,' he said, jumping up and leaving the room.

When he came back, he was carrying a folded sheet of paper which he handed to Diana.

'There was this,' he said in a meaningful tone.

The police officers watched her intently as she unfolded it and began to read. With a frozen expression, she pushed it across the table towards them.

Sergeant Allen came round to read it over his superior's shoulder.

Dear Diana, (he read)

I'm writing this in the car. All the way home I've been trying to decide what to do. Now my mind is made up. My life is in a sordid mess and I'm perched on a volcano which may erupt at any moment. In fact, it has already started to rumble. There'll probably be all sorts of rumours, but don't believe them all. I'm afraid I've not been a very good husband, though I've never been intentionally unkind. Anyway, I'm sure you'll cope somehow. My apologies and goodbye – G.

'I assume this is the judge's handwriting, Mrs Wenning?' Inspector Morrow said and, when Diana nodded, went on, 'I'll need to hand it to the coroner. It seems to make his intention clear enough, but what's he mean about being on a volcano that's about to erupt?'

'I've no idea, Inspector.' In a somewhat bleak tone she added, 'It obviously implies that he had troubles, but I certainly knew nothing about them. My daughter and son-in-law will be here shortly, I don't know whether they'll be able to cast any light on the matter. I'm completely in

64

the dark, but that's a wife's lot, isn't it? She's always supposed to be the last person to be aware of her husband's . . . her husband's outside behaviour.'

'Have you any reason to think there may have been another woman in his life?'

She gave a shrug of distaste. 'None until this moment, but now I don't know what to think. As I've said, I was unaware of anything.'

'Apart from his heavy drinking.'

'That hadn't yet become a serious problem, I assure you.'

Inspector Morrow gave a judicious nod. While he had been talking to Mrs Wenning, Detective Sergeant Allen had been re-reading the letter. He was struck by its language. It didn't contain a single spark of emotion. There was neither any expression of love or devotion for his wife nor of real regret for what he was doing to her. There wasn't even a note of self-pity. It was as perfunctory as a redundancy notice to a factory employee. Though he referred to troubles, he gave no hint as to their nature. On the other hand he clearly anticipated their disclosure after his death, hence the mention of probable rumours and the curt request that his wife shouldn't believe them all. That struck Terry Allen as a curious thing to say. The implication was that some, though not all, of the rumours might be true, but how was his wife expected to know which to reject? And what had he been up to to give rise to a whole tide of rumours?

Detective Sergeant Allen found himself considerably intrigued. The fact that judges were supposed to lead unblemished lives didn't mean that some of them hadn't strayed from time to time, but they had usually managed to do so with discretion so that their peccadilloes remained out of public view. It seemed, however, as if Judge Wenning's had been about to blow up in his face.

'We found a suitcase in the car, Mrs Wenning,' he said.

'I've brought it into the hall. May we open it and examine the contents?'

'It'll be my husband's day clothes. He took his dinner jacket with him yesterday and changed in town last night.'

'I'd still like to see for myself, Mrs Wenning.'

'All right, but please not in here.' She gave a small shiver.

'Perhaps W.P.C. Stokes can help me, sir,' he said to Inspector Morrow.

'Yes, go ahead, Sergeant, while I have a few further words with Mrs Wenning.'

'You have to hand it to Uncle Bernard, he's got a real bedside manner,' Terry Allen said as he and W.P.C. Stokes reached the hall. 'He'll probably have her tucked up in bed with an aspirin by the time we return.'

Sally Stokes smiled. 'I take it you want to search his suit pockets?' she said.

'Absolutely right.'

'What about his dinner-jacket pockets?'

'I went through those when Uncle Bernard and I were in the garage. There was only his wallet and some loose change and nothing of any significance in his wallet.'

'What are you expecting to find?'

'Everything or nothing. I just want to satisfy myself about their contents before others get looking.'

'His wife, you mean?'

'Or any of his family. There's always a tendency for relatives to cover up in these circumstances. The last thing they want is disagreeable publicity. I don't blame them, but it's not my job to assist.'

'And you believe there may be something nasty lurking in the woodshed?'

'Don't you? His suicide note said as much.'

'If my husband ever wrote me a farewell letter like that, I'd feel it was good riddance.'

'You're not married, are you?'

66

'No, but I shall be one day.'

'Ah! But I agree about the note. It wasn't exactly a tear-jerker.'

They had taken the suitcase into the drawing room and were kneeling in front of it on the floor. Terry Allen opened it and they found themselves looking at a jumble of not very neatly folded clothes.

'I wonder if he'd already decided to end his life when he stuffed these things in?' Sally Stokes remarked.

'Not being morbid, are you? Anyway, you can fold everything neatly when we put them back. Let's try his jacket pockets first.'

Kneeling beside Terry Allen and feeling the warmth of his body gave Sally a tingle of excitement that no amount of thoughts of duty could quell. She had always regarded him as being her type and the sudden intimate proximity of their bodies filled her with an erotic flight of fancy.

'You're trembling,' he said, giving her a quick glance. 'You're not going to faint, are you?'

'Of course not,' she replied with indignation.

'You'll have to get used to handling dead people's clothes.'

'It was nothing to do with that,' she said and edged slightly away.

He gave her a grin. 'Don't worry, I'm not about to rape you!'

'I'd like to see you try!' she replied, cross for having, as she felt, made herself ridiculous.

'Now let's see what's in these pockets!' he said, lifting the jacket of a black pin-stripe suit out of the case.

All, in fact, were empty save the left-hand pocket. From this he extracted a number of items which he started to examine one by one, observed by Sally Stokes.

There was a Bar point-to-point fixture list and another showing meetings at Sandown Park. An electricity bill for £268 had, from its appearance, been in his pocket for some time. There was a note from a fellow judge reminding him that he would be away for the first three days of the following week. There was also a folded sheet of paper on which were scrawled various names and figures.

'What do you make of that, Sally?' he asked handing her the piece of paper.

'Cloudburst,' she read out, with a frown. 'Mr Tapley, Himalayan Sprite . . . I know,' she exclaimed eagerly, 'they're names of horses.'

He nodded. 'And the figures refer to odds.'

'So the judge was a betting man.'

'A regular one, too, would be my guess. If we're right, we'll soon find out which races these horses were running in. Probably somewhere yesterday.'

He put the piece of paper on the floor beside him and picked up the last item which turned out to be the annual report and accounts of some legal society. As he unfolded the four stapled sheets of paper comprising the document an envelope fell out. He reached for it and stared at it hard for several seconds.

'Now this could be interesting,' he murmured, after peering inside and finding it empty. 'It's marked "Strictly private" and is addressed to the judge at court. Take a look!'

'It has a Gerrards Cross postmark,' she said.

'Yes, and someone has been very careful to disguise his handwriting. I wonder what was inside.' As he spoke, he picked up each of the other items again to make sure there was nothing hidden in their folds. 'My guess would be,' he went on, 'that he put the envelope in his pocket separately from its contents and it got tucked into this other bumph and overlooked when he turned his pocket out. I can think of no other reason why he should have kept the envelope and not what was inside it.' He paused. 'Some people tear up the envelopes and keep the letters; others

68

keep both. But I've yet to hear of anyone who only keeps the envelopes.'

'But what do you think he did with the contents?'

Terry Allen shrugged. 'Probably destroyed them.'

'So what's your theory?'

'That we have here the envelope of a blackmailing letter. They invariably look like this and are marked strictly private or personal or what have you. They also have this same calculatedly anonymous appearance.'

'I wonder who was blackmailing him?'

'Ah! Now that is a wide open question, but at least this envelope is a starting point. It's something to work on. We have a nice clear postmark and you'll note that it was only posted the day before yesterday, so memories will still be fresh.'

'Whose memories?' Sally asked in a tone of surprise.

'Everyone's. With luck we'll be able to find out in which box it was posted and when.'

'It mayn't actually have been a local person.'

Terry Allen nodded. 'And if it wasn't, there may be a better chance of somebody remembering having seen a stranger posting a letter in their road.'

'We're going to need a lot of luck.'

'Slogging routine with an occasional helping of luck, that's what detective work is. But the more I think about it, the more I feel I'm right. Just consider the time scale. He receives the letter at court yesterday morning, broods on it all day and finally decides there's only one way out, suicide.'

'He may have received previous letters.'

'Very likely. This one merely brought him to the end of the road.'

A car pulled up outside and a moment later a woman burst through the front door.

'Where's my mother?' she said, seemingly taking for granted the presence of two strangers in the drawing room.

'In the kitchen talking to Inspector Morrow. Would you be Mrs Wenning's daughter?'

'Yes. And this is my husband,' she said as a man joined her in the hall. 'Our name's Orden.'

She hurried off in the direction of the kitchen, but the man lingered.

'Did my father-in-law leave a note?' he enquired with more than casual interest. 'Incidentally, I take it you're police?'

Sergeant Allen made the necessary introductions and went on, 'Yes, he did. Said his life was in a mess and he was perched on a volcano which was about to erupt. Have you any idea what he meant, Mr Orden?'

'He had been drinking rather heavily of late,' Douglas Orden said in a weighty voice.

'So Mrs Wenning told us, but that hardly explains the note. Did he have other troubles?'

'He used to bet on horses. I think he may have had a few debts.'

'May have had?'

'Well, all right, he did. As a matter of fact I lent him money from time to time, but for heaven's sake don't tell my mother-in-law as she had no idea.'

'Did he repay the loans?'

Orden glanced slowly round the room as if to find the answer written on one of the drawing-room walls.

'I really don't think I ought to say anything more at the moment,' he replied, at length. 'It's purely a family matter and we'll doubtless want to consult our solicitor about what to say. I'm sure you understand, officer. Now, if you'll excuse me, I'd better go and find my wife.'

'What did I tell you!' Terry Allen said after Orden had gone. 'The family's prime interest in these cases is to cover up and keep the woodshed door firmly locked.' He gave Sally a cheerful smile. 'Want to come to the mortuary when we leave here?'

Not particularly.'

'I don't blame you. The post mortem can only confirm what we know, namely that he died from inhaling carbon-monoxide fumes.' He looked thoughtful. 'It's that envelope that really interests me.'

CHAPTER 10

Arthur Kedby was stunned by the news of Judge Wenning's suicide which he read in a Sunday paper.

He invariably enjoyed his Sundays, the late rising, the walk to the end of the street to buy papers and the leisurely breakfast that followed. In his case, of course, there was no reason why this couldn't be his daily routine as he had no regular job, but in that event he would no longer be able to savour his Sundays like the rest of the working population.

He had returned with two newspapers, each to satisfy a different need. The toast was under the grill, the kettle would soon give its cheerful whistle and his eggs were halfway through their three-minute boil when he picked up the more gossipy of the two papers.

The main front-page item was a report of scandalous goings-on after hours in a civil service canteen and he decided he must give it closer attention after he had eaten. After all, scandalous goings-on were his basic raw material.

He was about to lay down the paper and attend to his breakfast when his eye became riveted. *Judge in horror death shock*, he read. The report went on: *Judge Gerald Wenning was yesterday found dead in his car in the garage of his elegant Gerrards Cross home. Known for his* bon viveur *style, he was dressed in his dinner jacket when*

72

found by his wife who told reporters that her husband had attended a dinner in London the previous evening. The police said it was a case of apparent suicide and it is understood that a note was left, though its contents have not been disclosed. An inquest will be held. Your reporter later learnt that a length of hose pipe had been connected from the exhaust to the interior of the car. Judge Wenning, who sat at West Middlesex Court, was known for his stern views on all types of hooliganism, often deploring the abolition of corporal punishment for youthful offenders.

Only the acrid smell of burning toast brought Arthur back to reality. His eggs, too, had become as inedible as squash balls.

In no mood to start cooking again, he made do with coffee and a slice of bread and butter.

His initial sense of shock was replaced by frustration and annoyance. All that trouble for nothing – and now he was back to square one with a depleted bank balance and no immediate prospect of replenishing it. Moreover, his impending fiftieth birthday which he viewed with despair was that much closer.

When he had finished his meal he lit one of the small cigars he smoked at times of stress and sat down to think.

What he would dearly like to know was the nature of the note Wenning had left, but there seemed no prospect of finding that out in advance of the inquest and by then the information would probably be valueless. He would be very surprised if the judge had made any specific mention of his escapades with Tony Ching. That was a secret he would clearly wish to take with him to the grave.

Thinking along these lines, Arthur also reckoned that he would have destroyed the two blackmailing letters, seeing that they contained implicit references to his conduct.

But even if the letters were still in evidence, Arthur was unable to see how they could possibly be traced back to him. All they could do was inform the small circle who read them that Judge Wenning had behaved in a most unjudgelike manner.

A moment later, however, this thought was pushed aside by a less agreeable one. In his second letter he had referred to 'our late Chinese friend' and if that were to be linked with Tony Ching, it could bring police enquiries uncomfortably close.

On the other hand, why should he, Arthur, come under particular scrutiny? He wasn't the only person who knew about the comings and goings of the basement flat. Even so, he fervently hoped that his two letters would not fall into police hands and, indeed, was able to persuade himself of the unlikelihood of this happening. He was left feeling, however, like a dog whose bone has been rudely snatched away.

Later that day he noticed Greg talking to someone at the top of the basement steps. He waited until he saw him go down to his flat and then telephoned.

'It's Arthur, Greg. I was just calling to see how you were.'

'Oh, I'm all right, thanks,' Greg said in a distracted voice.

'You're not moving yet?'

'No. I'll probably hang on a bit longer. I still don't know what to do. Friends tell me that I ought to make a complete break. I may go abroad. Spain, America, somewhere like that,' he said, as though the world was a jumble of countries.

'Have the police been in touch with you again?'

'Chief Inspector Pennerly phoned me last week. It was to do with sending Tony's bits and pieces to his mother in Hong Kong. He wanted to know if I'd pay. Well, it depended how much, I said and then he said . . .'

'Did he say how the enquiry was going?' Arthur broke in, fearing an otherwise tedious and interminable saga on the subject of the disposal of Tony's belongings.

'He said they were still busy interviewing people, but I didn't get the impression they were making any progress. If you ask me, they'll never catch the chap unless he strikes again and perhaps not even then.'

On this dour note, Arthur rang off and decided to go for a walk in Kensington Gardens. The sun was out and the autumn colours would lift his spirits. And, indeed, by the time he returned home, he felt that he had the various possibilities arising from Judge Wenning's suicide in clearer perspective and was, accordingly, more cheerful.

It was a state of mind which was to last for another three days before being shattered.

Before that, however (on the Tuesday, in fact), Arthur brought off a minor coup which pleased him and showed that he still had his wits about him. He had gone into a small self-service store and been quick to notice that the girl cashier was obviously distracted and inattentive. She wrong-changed the two customers ahead of him, so that when his turn came he was able to persuade her that he had proffered a £10 note when, in fact, he had handed over £5. She had been a bit suspicious at first, but he had been so politely insistent that she accepted his word and gave him the additional change.

Then in the middle of Thursday afternoon his telephone rang and a neutral voice said, 'Is that Mr Kedby?'

'Yes, speaking.'

'I'm calling on behalf of Detective Chief Inspector Pennerly. He just wanted to be sure that you were at home before coming round to see you. He'll be with you shortly.'

'Shortly' turned out to be exactly three minutes and Arthur was later to reflect on the devious cunning of the ploy. They had not wanted to turn up in an ostentatious display of strength only to discover he was out, but, having ascertained he was in, they obviously hoped to catch him unawares by the speed of their arrival, perhaps in a panicky disposal of telltale evidence of some sort. They must have been waiting in the car just round the corner until informed over their radio that he was at home.

At all events, it seemed to Arthur that he had barely put down the receiver and gone across to the window when their car pulled up outside the house with a pneumatic lurch. He noticed Pennerly gaze up at the window as he jumped out. From the other side of the car a young man with straight blond hair leapt out and hurried round to join Pennerly who was bounding up the porch steps.

A second later, Arthur's bell rang.

''Afternoon, Mr Kedby,' Pennerly said unsmilingly when Arthur opened his front door. 'This is Detective Sergeant Allen of Thames Valley police,' he went on, indicating the blond-haired young man at his side. 'All right if we come in?'

Arthur didn't know whether to be relieved or not that the driver had remained outside in the car. Passers-by always seemed to show greater curiosity in a parked police car in which someone was sitting. On the other hand, three policemen in his bed-sitter would have been even more oppressive.

'Thames Valley police, did you say?' he enquired in a faintly puzzled tone.

'That's right,' Pennerly said briskly, giving Sergeant Allen a nodded cue.

'Have you ever been to Gerrards Cross, Mr Kedby?' Allen asked.

Arthur felt his senses reeling, but knew that he must not show any outward sign of perturbation.

'Gerrards Cross?' he repeated stupidly. 'Have I ever been to Gerrards Cross, you ask?'

'It would seem a perfectly simple and straightforward question,' Pennerly remarked. 'One that can actually be answered by a plain yes or no.'

'It seems such an extraordinary question to ask out of

the blue,' he replied, trying desperately to reassemble his mental processes.

'Sergeant Allen wouldn't ask it without a reason,' Pennerly said.

'May I ask what is the reason?'

'I suggest you just answer the question.' Pennerly's voice had a steely note.

'I've certainly been through Gerrards Cross,' Arthur said cautiously. 'Before the M40 was opened, one drove through it on the way to Oxford and the Cotswolds.'

'When were you last there, sir?' Allen asked, declining to be drawn into a discussion on England's highways.

'I don't recall being there very recently,' Arthur said, after (to him) an agonising pause.

'Would you have been there within the last two weeks?'

Arthur took a deep breath. It would be fatal to be caught out with a provable lie. Equivocation and further equivocation must be his line of defence to these brutally pertinent questions.

'As a matter of fact, I did drive through there about two weeks ago. I hired a car to have a day in the country.'

'Where did you go?'

'I turned off the main road west of High Wycombe, parked the car and went for a long walk, which was the main object of my trip. I felt I needed a breath of proper country air.'

'And you drove through Gerrards Cross.'

'I must have done, not that it made any impression on me at the time.'

'Why didn't you take the M40 that bypasses the town?'

Arthur gave the officers a nervous smile. 'Not being a regular driver, I'm afraid I avoid motorways. In fact, they terrify me. All those huge lorries, and cars flashing past far faster than I want to drive. Moreover, if one's having an outing into the countryside, motorways are the last place one wants to be.'

'Did you stop in Gerrards Cross?'

'No. As I explained, I don't actually recall driving through, but I obviously did.'

'Might you have stopped for petrol?'

Arthur shook his head. 'No. I didn't fill up until I got back to London.'

'So you never got out of the car in Gerrards Cross?'

'No–o.'

'You're sure about that, sir?'

'Quite certain.' Equivocation had to end at some point and the alternative answer would have opened up a whole succession of awkward questions.

'What was the date you rented this car?'

'Let me think! It must have been two weeks ago today.'

'And the name of the hire firm?'

'Jolly's in Gloucester Road.'

Sergeant Allen glanced across at Chief Inspector Pennerly who had been listening with the air of a moderator.

'I expect you've been thinking about Tony Ching's death since we last spoke, Mr Kedby?' he now said.

'Naturally, I've thought about it. I've been wondering how your enquiries are going?'

'Slowly. All we need now is a break and I have a feeling we're going to get one soon.'

'I'm glad to hear it,' Arthur said, with a hollow sensation in the pit of his stomach. He was feeling utterly unnerved by the police visitation.

'I'm sure you must have thought of something further which might help our enquiries, Mr Kedby?'

'I'm afraid not. The people in the flat immediately above Tony Ching's would have been much more likely to have heard something. Even the woman who lives in the neighbouring basement flat.'

'But you knew him, Mr Kedby. These other people didn't. You were on friendly terms with him. You were aware of his goings-on.'

Arthur frowned, unsure of the precise implication of Pennerly's words, but not caring for the trend of the conversation.

'Nevertheless, I'm afraid there's nothing further I can tell you. I didn't hear anything and I didn't see anyone.'

'Tell me about the people who used to visit Tony for so-called massage. What sort were they for the most part? Middle-aged? Respectably dressed? Give me some idea.'

'As I told you, Chief Inspector, when you were last here, I didn't make a point of keeping watch on his visitors and on the occasions when I did see someone arriving, they were usually behaving so furtively that one scarcely caught a glimpse of a face. And when they were leaving, all one saw was a retreating back.'

'Were they mostly well dressed?'

'I didn't notice their dress, so I really can't tell you.'

'Well-to-do types, were they?'

'My general impression was that they were mostly middle-aged and could have been anything from bus drivers to bank managers.'

'By bank managers, I take it you mean men who were respectable and prosperous in appearance.'

'Certainly some of them were,' Arthur said, uncomfortably aware that he was being drawn ever further along a path he had no wish to tread.

'I suppose some of them might have been priests or lawyers?'

'I never saw anyone arrive wearing a dog collar,' Arthur said with a tentative smile.

'No, I don't imagine they'd be quite as brazen as that. Any more than, say, a judge would come wearing a wig.'

Arthur blinked and stared stupidly at Chief Inspector Pennerly.

'You look as if you've seen a ghost, Mr Kedby.'

'It's just that I don't know what to make of your bizarre suggestions.'

'About the possibility of parsons and lawyers having visited Tony? Come, Mr Kedby, you know as well as I do that that particular predilection recognises no barriers, either class or social. Tony would certainly not have been the first of his kind if he'd had a judge or a member of parliament among his clients.'

'I wouldn't know,' Arthur said stiffly.

'I wonder if I might use your phone?' Pennerly said. 'I'd like to call my station. It won't take a moment.' He gave Arthur a half-smile. 'I'll even pay for it if you wish.'

'Help yourself.'

Arthur watched him dial a number and heard him ask to speak to Sergeant Cottingham.

'They've arrived, have they? Fine, well, we'll be back shortly. Keep everyone happy until we arrive.' He exchanged a glance with Detective Sergeant Allen, then turning to Arthur said abruptly, 'Do you have an envelope I could borrow, Mr Kedby?'

'What sort of envelope?'

'Just an ordinary cheap one if you have such a thing.'

Arthur went across to the corner cupboard in which he kept his writing materials.

'This do?' he asked, holding up a square white envelope.

'Do you have any self-adhesive ones?'

'No, I don't.'

He wished his reply hadn't sounded quite so defiant, but he was viewing their visit with increasing alarm. The questions about Gerrards Cross had been unnerving enough, but this seemingly casual request for an envelope had really thrown him, as it was doubtless intended to do. What had they found out which prompted such a sinister interest in him? He knew he had to muster his scattered wits and keep them sharply about him. The request for the envelope seemed to indicate that they had found at least one of those in which he had posted his letters to the judge.

But how had they managed to link Judge Wenning with Tony Ching? For they, indeed, appeared to have done so. Perhaps it was no more than guesswork. But the most uncomfortable question of all was why should suspicion have fallen on him, Arthur Kedby?

'You wouldn't mind accompanying me back to the station, would you, Mr Kedby?' Pennerly asked, as if it were a completely reasonable request. 'It won't take long and we have a car outside,' he added, as if to clinch the matter.

'I certainly would mind, unless you give me an explanation,' Arthur said with greater spirit than he actually felt.

'Sergeant Allen will tell you on the way. You've said you'd wish to help our enquiries and I'm sure you meant it, didn't you, Mr Kedby?'

'Of course, but . . .'

'That's fine, then. You go on down with him and I'll follow you in a few moments. I'd just like to use your bathroom. Give me your keys and I'll lock the front door behind me.'

Arthur felt pole-axed by the sheer effrontery of the suggestion.

'How do I know you won't search my flat behind my back?'

Pennerly looked thoughtful for a moment.

'You don't, of course, but would you object if I did?'

'Most certainly I should. As a matter of principle.'

'Ah! Only as a matter of principle?'

'Yes.'

'Not because you're afraid I might find something?'

'You won't find anything incriminating here, if that's what you mean.'

'Incriminating, Mr Kedby? Incriminating in what way?'

'In any way.'

'But you must have had something specific in mind

81

when you used that word. Didn't it strike you that way, Sergeant Allen?'

'Yes, sir.'

'So, Mr Kedby?'

'I've already said. In anything at all. And, anyway, how do I know you won't plant something when I'm not here?' Arthur asked truculently. When your back is really against the wall, counter-attack is the only option.

Pennerly contrived to look pained. 'What do you have in mind, a bit of cannabis beneath a cushion?'

'If you really wish to visit the bathroom, there's the door and I'll wait here,' Arthur said stonily.

Pennerly shrugged. 'Are you sure you can trust me not to plant something in the cistern? It's always been a favoured hiding-place.'

He walked across to the cupboard-sized bathroom and closed the door behind him. Arthur felt that he had, at least, won that round. He was certain that what Pennerly had really wanted was to search for an envelope that matched those in which he had sent his letters to Judge Wenning. Not that he would have been successful, anyway, thanks to Arthur's precautions.

'Well, are we ready to go?' Pennerly asked, emerging from the bathroom.

'I've decided that I won't come unless you give me a reason,' Arthur said in a resolute tone.

'Perhaps you'd better tell Mr Kedby, Sergeant.'

'We want you to take part in an identification parade.'

Arthur felt his throat contract and his heart start to pound again.

'How do you mean, take part?'

'You answer the description of a man seen in Gerrards Cross on two recent separate occasions.'

'Is that a crime?'

'You've told us you only drove through without stopping. We'd like to know if certain witnesses are able to identify you as someone they saw walking in the town.'

'And supposing they do, what does that prove?' Arthur asked in a shaky voice.

'For one thing, it would show you to be a liar,' Pennerly remarked.

'I still don't understand what I'm supposed to have done. You can hardly expect me to take part in an identification parade just to satisfy some police whim or other. What's it matter whether or not I was ever in Gerrards Cross?'

'All right, Mr Kedby, there's no need to shout,' Pennerly said. 'People are often asked to attend identification parades in the course of an enquiry. I assure you there's nothing unusual about the request.'

'And if these witnesses, whoever they are, pick me out as someone they think they saw in Gerrards Cross, what's it prove?'

'It goes to show that you were somewhere you've denied being.'

'And where does that take you?' Arthur asked with increasing agitation.

Pennerly appeared to weigh up his answer. Then fixing Arthur with a thoughtful look, he said, 'It takes me some way towards proving a charge of murder against you. Incidentally, Mr Kedby, what do you do for a living?'

'I have a small private income,' Arthur said stiffly.

'You don't have any regular job?' Pennerly remarked, casting him a quizzical glance.

Arthur shook his head. He was tempted to add that he did occasional free-lance work, but could see this would plunge him into dangerous waters.

CHAPTER 11

Arthur scarcely heard what the uniformed inspector in charge of the parade was saying to him. He knew that its procedure was being explained, but his mind had become so numb as to be incapable of normal assimilation.

He glanced at the others who had been assembled for the parade and was conscious of reflecting that they looked as nondescript as himself. He selected a place more or less in the middle of the line as offering greater refuge than either end.

'Just try and relax,' the inspector said in a bluffly kind tone. 'If you look all nervous and tense, it can be a bit of a giveaway. Here, have this piece of gum, it'll stop your teeth chattering.'

He departed to fetch the first witness, leaving Arthur feeling as if he was about to have all his teeth extracted without an anaesthetic.

He realised bitterly that he, who had so often lived successfully outside the law, was wholly unprepared for his first major confrontation with its guardians. The visitation of Pennerly and the blond-haired sergeant had completely undermined his morale. Their velvet-gloved assault had been quite as effective as the physical ill-treatment meted out by the less humane interrogators of some other countries.

84

But somehow he must gather his wits together, as he would certainly need them during whatever came after the parade.

He ought to have demanded a lawyer, but Pennerly had a way of gently steam-rollering anything that didn't suit his purpose.

He became aware of the first witness coming out of a door to his right and immediately fixed his gaze straight ahead with the steadfastness of a guardsman on parade.

A few seconds later a woman appeared in his line of vision and stared at him with ferocious intensity. It was the same woman who had popped her head over the neighbouring fence when he was quietly reconnoitring the Wennings' garden. She moved on down the line, but returned to point at Arthur and declare loudly, 'That's the man.'

'Tough luck,' said the man on Arthur's right. 'Better change your position.'

Arthur did so, but with the air of someone making a small detour on his way to the gallows.

The other two witnesses turned out to be the boys he had seen giggling as he emerged from the railway station on his second visit to Gerrards Cross and whom he had noticed again on his return to the station when they had been gazing into a shop window.

On this occasion each looked mildly nervous, but with unmistakable eagerness beneath their faintly anxious exteriors. The first showed some diffidence in picking out Arthur, but the second none at all.

After they had left the scene, the inspector made a small speech of thanks to those who had so public-spiritedly given their time to participate in the cause of justice and Arthur was led to a room where Detective Chief Inspector Pennerly and Detective Sergeant Allen were waiting.

'I expect you could do with a cup of tea?' Pennerly said agreeably. 'Cigarette?'

Arthur was thankful to accept both, even though it was rare for him to smoke a cigarette. But in his present state nothing which might help to calm his nerves was to be rejected.

'So all three witnesses picked you out, Mr Kedby,' Pennerly went on. 'What do you have to say about that?'

'They're mistaken.'

'You weren't aware of ever having seen any of them before?'

'No, and I don't even know where they're supposed to have seen me.'

'I'd have expected you to ask that before alleging they were mistaken.'

'I assume they think they saw me in Gerrards Cross,' Arthur said, trying to retrieve his slip.

Pennerly turned to Sergeant Allen.

'You'd better tell Mr Kedby who they were; or should I say remind him?'

'Mrs Barker lives next door to Judge and Mrs Wenning,' Allen said. 'She identified you as a man she saw on the private footpath which runs between their properties. She says that the man in question was showing great interest in the Wennings' house and garden.'

Arthur shook his head as if to disclaim responsibility for other people's aberrations.

'She says that she spoke to this man and asked him what he was doing there,' Allen went on.

'Well, it wasn't me. I've never heard of Judge Wenning.'

'He committed suicide last week,' Pennerly broke in. 'Don't you read the newspapers?'

'I believe I did read something about a judge being found dead in his car, but I didn't take in the name.'

'Or the place?'

'What place?'

'Gerrards Cross, Mr Kedby.'

86

'I'm afraid I don't share your interest in Gerrards Cross.'

'And the two boys,' Allen continued, 'identified you as the man they observed leaving the railway station, walking to the post office where he posted a letter and then returning immediately to the station.'

'I've never heard of anything so ridiculous, so . . . so contrived,' Arthur stammered, feeling the blood drain from his face.

But Sergeant Allen hadn't finished. 'They had seen a programme on television about surveillance and were putting the art into practice. You happened to be one of their targets. On your way back to the station, they pretended to be looking into a shop window but were, in fact, watching your reflection all the time.'

'Why did you go all the way to Gerrards Cross to post a letter, Mr Kedby?'

'It wasn't me. How many more times do I have to tell you?'

'So all three witnesses are quite mistaken?'

'They must be.'

'Either that or you're lying,' Pennerly remarked.

'Why should I lie?'

'I can think of several reasons for that, though they all boil down to one. You're in big trouble and people in that position invariably try and lie their way out of it.'

'Perhaps you'd like to tell me what sort of trouble I'm supposed to be in?'

'Certainly. I believe that you and Tony were blackmailing Judge Wenning as a result of an indiscreet visit he had paid to Tony. I believe that subsequently you and Tony fell out and that you murdered him. That's what I believe happened, Mr Kedby, and that's what I expect to be able to prove.'

Arthur felt as if he had received a succession of hard punches to the solar plexus.

'You're crazy,' he said faintly. 'It's a complete fabrication. I demand to see my lawyer.'

'All in good time. Let's first try and find out what we *can* agree about. For example, I take it you would agree that it would be most unusual for someone to go all the way from London to Gerrards Cross by train just to post a letter?'

'I can't answer hypothetical questions.'

'Unless of course that person had some very special reason for posting it in that particular town?' Pennerly went on, as if Arthur hadn't spoken.

And so the interview continued, with Arthur denying, blocking and stone-walling each fresh line of interrogation. As time passed, it became clear to him that Pennerly lacked sufficient evidence to prefer a charge. The fact that it would have been an utterly false charge tended to diminish the small degree of comfort he would otherwise have been afforded. That he stood in peril of being charged with a murder he hadn't committed was quite horrific. He hadn't previously believed that such things could happen.

It was towards the end of the interview, in the course of which he had at some point been cautioned, that Detective Sergeant Allen suddenly handed him a ballpoint pen and a piece of paper.

'I'd like you to print something on that piece of paper for me, Mr Kedby. Capital letters. You understand? Ready? Judge Gerald Wenning, West Middlesex Crown Court, Uxbridge.'

Arthur had known what was coming before Allen had even begun to dictate.

It was shortly after this that both men left the room and a young P.C. came in and sat on a chair by the door.

When the two officers returned, Pennerly said, 'Well, that's all for the moment, Mr Kedby, though I shall want to see you again before long so don't disappear.'

'You mean I can go home?'

'Yes. I'll even arrange for a car to take you.'

No sooner was Arthur back in his flat than he drew the curtains to exclude the hateful world outside, poured himself a large brandy and went to lie down on his bed.

The whole episode had been a complete nightmare, but what now remained most clearly fixed in his mind was Pennerly's quietly confident assertion: 'I believe *you* murdered him and that's what I expect to be able to prove.'

CHAPTER 12

Diana Wenning went and stayed with her daughter and son-in-law until after her husband's funeral. Christine had suggested she should remain longer, but she felt it was time to return home and attend to the aftermath of her husband's death.

Everyone had been kind and tactful, but each day seemed to bring a fresh slant on aspects of his life.

First, Christine had broken to her the news of his gambling debts.

'I wish you didn't have to know, Mummy, but I feel I must tell you so that you're not taken by surprise if his assets turn out to be rather less than you expected.'

The major shock had been to discover that he had been borrowing money from his son-in-law.

'Don't worry about the loans Douglas made,' Christine had said. 'The last thing he would want is to add to your worries by claiming on the estate as a creditor.'

'But of course he must be repaid,' Diana had replied and been conscious that Douglas himself had not dissented.

Indeed, her son-in-law had seemed morose and taciturn for most of her stay with them.

'With hindsight, however,' she had gone on, 'I rather wish you hadn't helped him out. It might have been better if he had been made to face reality at the outset. I'd always known he was fond of gambling, but I had absolutely no idea that he'd been incurring these terrible losses and borrowing from his own son-in-law. It explains why he sought refuge in drink.' After a sigh she added, 'Well, at least, the house must be worth a great deal. I shall sell it and use the money to pay off his debts. In any event, it would be far too big for me on my own and I'll need something smaller.'

It was at this point she had noticed Christine cast her husband a worried glance. It was enough to make Diana say, 'I take it the freehold is still unencumbered; Gerald didn't sign it away to raise money?'

'I'm afraid he did offer it as security,' Douglas said gruffly. 'It was his idea that my loans to him should be secured by way of a mortgage.'

'Do you know whether anyone else holds mortgages on the property?' she had asked a trifle bleakly. Douglas had given a vague shrug and she had said, 'Well, I shall doubtless find out soon enough.'

On her drive home the day after the funeral, which had been kept quiet and unpublicised, she reflected on her new status of widowhood. She had never been a particularly emotional woman and her marriage had soon become a dutiful partnership in which she made most of the adjustments and accommodations.

From being a rather dashing and handsome young barrister, Gerald had turned into a selfish and vaguely discontented man of middle years. Being appointed a judge had satisfied his ego for a time, but it had not been long before he was complaining about the tedium of much of the work with which he had to deal.

Diana had always realised that, at the root of their uninspired relationship, lay their differing attitudes towards sex. Put briefly, he was oversexed and she, once the novelty had worn off, had taken little pleasure in it.

It was on the day after her return home that Detective Sergeant Allen called on her.

He had the anxious air of a young man about to face a tricky interview board. She took him into the drawing room and offered him a cup of coffee which he accepted with alacrity.

'Do smoke if you want to,' she said.

'I don't, Mrs Wenning,' he replied, running a hand over his straight blond hair which looked as smooth as the coat of a long-haired Persian cat.

'Well, sit down and I'll fetch the coffee.'

When she returned to the room, he was still standing. She didn't recall his looking so nervous the first time they met, but perhaps that was because on that occasion it had been she who had been in a state of nerves.

'I had hoped to bring Woman Police Constable Stokes with me,' he said, 'but at the last minute she was whisked off on another matter.'

'Was she the young woman who accompanied you that morning my husband was found?'

'Yes. We've been working together on the case.' He took a sip of coffee and cleared his throat. 'Mrs Wenning, in the note which he left, your husband described his life as having become a mess. Have you found out what he was referring to?'

'I've discovered that he had considerable debts, mostly as a result of gambling.'

Sergeant Allen nodded. 'We think that he was also being blackmailed.'

'Over his debts, do you mean? I suppose that, as a judge, he'd have been vulnerable to blackmail if he borrowed money unwisely.'

'We think he was being blackmailed over something else. Over a sexual matter.'

To Terry Allen's relief, she reacted neither with tears

92

nor with a show of indignation. She merely put her head on one side and waited for him to continue.

Before he did so, he took another sip of coffee. Though only twenty-four, he had come, after six years in the police, to regard himself as hardened to most things. But to have to explain to a woman who was old enough to be his mother, and was a judge's widow to boot, that her husband had been involved in homosexual activities was the most embarrassing assignment he could recall. Moreover, he wasn't really sure that it would have been made any easier if W.P.C. Stokes had been able to accompany him.

Focusing a wary eye on her, he went on, 'We believe he visited a Chinese boy in the Earls Court district.'

'Boy, did you say?' she asked, with an expression of revulsion.

'Yes. I'm afraid it must come as a great shock to you.'

'How old was this boy?'

'In his twenties.'

'Oh, that sort of a boy,' she said with a small sigh of relief. 'I thought, at first, you meant a child. How long had it been going on?'

'We've no idea. The boy concerned is dead. He was murdered.'

'Surely, you're not suggesting that my husband . . .'

'No, no,' Allen broke in hastily. 'We believe the murderer was the same man who was blackmailing your husband.'

'How sordid it all sounds! What made you connect my husband with this Chinese boy?'

'We found his telephone number at the back of your husband's pocket diary. It was one of two numbers that had no name beside it, which made us wonder.'

'Whose was the other number?'

'A Dutch boy's.'

'Another male prostitute, do you mean?'

'I'm afraid so. In the Bayswater area.'

93

'I don't see that you need be apologetic.'

'I realise how you must feel, Mrs Wenning.'

She gave him a small sad smile. 'It's sweet of you to say that and I appreciate it, but, how shall I put it, I'm not totally surprised; at least, not in the way you may expect. You see, my husband liked variety in his sexual life, he was naturally promiscuous, as are so many men. I'm aware that he was unfaithful to me on at least two occasions, and there were doubtless others I knew nothing about. The two I did find out about belonged to the call-girl category. Looking back, I can see it had to be only a matter of time before he tired of straightforward sex and wanted to try something different. What does surprise me, however, is that he was foolhardy enough to court all the risks involved in visiting a male prostitute. If he had ever been found out, it'd have been the end of his career as a judge.' She stopped abruptly. 'But he was discovered, wasn't he? Hence the blackmail followed by his death.'

'I gather you had no idea he was visiting such people?'

'None. Any more than I knew about his gambling debts.'

'Have you found anything in the course of going through his papers that might have a bearing on what we've been discussing?'

'I haven't yet had an opportunity. I went to stay with my daughter and son-in-law immediately after his death and I returned home only yesterday. If I do come across anything, I'll let you know, but I doubt whether I shall. My husband would have been unlikely to keep anything here that could have proved an embarrassment to him if discovered. What about his room at court, has that been searched?'

'The clerk has put all his personal belongings in a cupboard.'

'Has anyone looked through them?'

'The police certainly haven't,' Allen said promptly.

'I wasn't going to make any accusations. Indeed, you're at liberty to do so as far as I'm concerned.'

He tried to conceal his surprise. Contrary to what he had said to Sally Stokes, there seemed to be no question of a family cover-up so far as Mrs Wenning was concerned.

'Would you mind phoning the court and saying that you have no objection to my going through his personal effects?' he said eagerly.

She frowned and for a moment Terry Allen feared she was having second thoughts. But then she said, 'Yes, I'll do that, but first I'd like you to make me a promise as I feel I can trust you. Please don't officially disclose anything you find without first having a word with me. Will you do that?'

'If you phone the court now, Mrs Wenning, I'll drive there straight away and call you back as soon as I've made my search.'

Less than two hours later he was back at the house bearing a small but stout metal cash-box. He had already phoned Diana Wenning from the court to say that he would be returning.

'There was nothing apart from this,' he said, holding out the cash-box. 'I asked the clerk of the court if he had any idea of the contents, but neither he nor anyone else had ever seen it open. I gather Judge Wenning kept it in a locked drawer of his desk.' He gave it a small shake. 'It's got something in it. I believe your husband's keys were returned to you with other items taken from him at the mortuary.'

'If you wait a moment, I'll fetch them.' When she returned to the drawing room, she handed him a ring with about half a dozen keys on it. 'You open it,' she said.

The second key he tried turned in the lock and he lifted the lid to reveal a wad of papers. Many seemed to be bookmakers' accounts and other tokens of his indebtedness. At the bottom, however, was an envelope which Terry

95

Allen at once recognised as being identical to the one that had been found in his jacket pocket. He took in the date and the WC2 postmark, but was chagrined to find it empty. On turning it over, he saw that there was writing on the reverse side and his interest immediately quickened.

£5000.

John Smith, Trafalgar Square P.O.

£200 a month.

'Is that your husband's writing, Mrs Wenning?' he asked.

'Yes, but what does it mean?'

'My guess would be that it's a summary of the contents of the envelope. That your husband destroyed the original letter, but made a brief note of what was in it.'

'But who's John Smith?'

'That's something I shall try and find out,' he said eagerly, as he pushed away a lock of straight hair that had fallen over his forehead. 'May I use your telephone to call Detective Chief Inspector Penneriy at Kensington?'

Diana nodded and watched him cross the room. She was sure Christine and Douglas would disapprove of her over-ready co-operation with the police. She might even regret it later herself, but for the moment she was consumed by a feeling of almost masochistic abandonment.

Let the whole world know the sort of man her husband had been! What did she care! Why, they might even have made a *ménage à trois*, she, Gerald and the Chinese boy!

She let out a small shriek of laughter as the thought came to her and then hurried from the room to give way to the flood of tears she was no longer able to hold back.

CHAPTER 13

The day after his mother-in-law's departure, Douglas Orden drove up to London. He left home at half past seven and told his wife that he expected to be back by six o'clock.

'Is there any way I can get in touch with you if need arises?' she asked as she accompanied him to the garage. Very often he left her a telephone number, but didn't seem about to do so on this occasion.

He puckered his lips and, after a second's hesitation, said, 'I'll be moving around most of the day, so it'll be better if I call you. Not that anything's likely to arise.'

'Probably not, darling, but you know I always like to consult you if I'm in doubt about lowering a price or something of that sort.'

'Then I'll call you around twelve if that'll make you happier.'

Giving her a quick kiss, he got into the car and backed out of the garage. Christine watched him with a troubled expression. He had been strangely preoccupied since her father's death and had reacted tetchily when she had tried to find out what was on his mind. She felt certain that his mood was related to the money her father had borrowed and not repaid and she had begun to wonder whether it might not be more than Douglas had let on. There was no doubt that it had become an embarrassment to all concerned, not least her unfortunate mother, who now found herself involved willy-nilly.

She returned to the house, the front part of which had been adapted as a shop and embarked on her round of domestic duty. They had been married for three years and Christine thought the time had come to start a family, but Douglas was less keen.

'Let's wait a bit longer, darling,' he said when she had recently broached the subject again.

'Well, not too long,' she replied, 'or you'll be forty before the baby arrives.'

'Hey, don't age me prematurely. I'm only thirty-five.'

'I want to have our first before I'm thirty.'

'That's still five years ahead.'

'I know, but procrastination can become a habit.'

'I promise it won't.'

That conversation had taken place not long before her father's death. Since that event she hadn't felt like bringing the matter up again.

It had been as a result of working as a secretary to a London antiques dealer that she had met Douglas. She had accompanied her boss to a country sale where he had been after some Georgian silver, only to be outbid, to his intense annoyance, by her future husband. Douglas had later disclosed to her that he already had a client who was prepared to pay whatever was necessary to secure the silver. By the time she came to marry him, a year after their first meeting, she had learnt quite a bit about the trade, not all of which appealed to her sense of what was honest.

'It's a real crafty world,' Douglas was fond of saying. 'You need to have your wits about you all the time.'

So far as Christine was aware, they made a good living out of the business. At least, there never seemed to be any shortage of money. She was never sure, however, that she was necessarily told the whole story behind some of their acquisitions.

'I wouldn't want to shock my little judge's daughter,' Douglas was given to saying in a playful tone.

At about the moment she completed the household chores, he was driving through London's western suburbs. A few miles farther on, he turned off the main road in the direction of Ealing where Ron and Percy Sugarman lived within a hundred yards of one another in Mycroft Road.

Percy was the younger of the two brothers by three years and also the more extrovert, though there was little to choose between them when it came to physical toughness. As from time to time their operations took them outside the law, they needed to be able to look after themselves.

They now lived with their respective wives on the west side of London, but had originated in the East End where family loyalties could often show a violent face.

Douglas had been told to come to Percy's house as Ron had the builders at his constructing a sun parlour. As he parked his car and approached the front door, he could hear a flow of stilted Spanish coming from inside. It ceased as soon as he pressed the bell and a few seconds later, Percy opened the door.

' 'Ello, Doug, come on in. I was just brushing up on the old Spanish as Lorraine and I are going off to our villa for Christmas. You know Ron's bought one now, don't you? It's about ten miles up the coast from our place. 'Is 'asn't got a pool, but 'e's going to 'ave one put in. 'E'll be 'ere in a moment.'

He led the way into the living room and walked across to a small bar in one corner.

'What'll you 'ave, Doug? Beer, brandy? Or I can even fix you up with a glass of champagne. The proper stuff, not your fizzy piss.'

'I'd prefer a cup of coffee.'

'O.K., coffee it shall be. I told Lorraine to leave some on the side before she went out. Just sit down and make yourself at 'ome while I fetch it.'

While he was out of the room, Douglas heard a car pull up outside and a few seconds later Ron walked in.

' 'Morning, Doug,' he said, glancing round the room. 'Where's Percy?'

'In the kitchen.'

Ron Sugarman strolled over to the bar and surveyed the array of bottles with a frown. Then reaching beneath the counter, he brought out a can of beer.

'Thought I 'eard you arrive,' Percy said, as he returned to the room carrying a mug of coffee which he handed to Douglas. 'I've sugared it. O.K.?'

'Doesn't matter. I can still drink it.'

'If you two have finished, let's start, shall we?' Ron said morosely, sitting down opposite Douglas. 'So what's the situation?'

'Regarding my father-in-law's debts, do you mean?'

' 'E certainly didn't do us a service by doing 'imself in like that,' Percy remarked. 'Ron and I reckon 'e owes us twenty-one thousand quid and what we'd like to know, Doug, is when are we going to see it?'

'Exactly,' said Ron.

'I'm afraid it'll be some time before his estate is settled. You know how long these things always take.'

'And what are we expected to do in the meantime?' Ron enquired with a hint of menace in his tone.

'I can only ask you to be patient. My mother-in-law still doesn't know about the loans you made or the extent of her husband's indebtedness. In any event, your names don't appear on any bits of paper. That's why we formed Mycroft Investments Limited so that you could make the loans behind a front.'

'That's not telling us anything new,' Ron said. 'We lent the money because you asked us to.'

'And because we always like to 'elp a friend when we can,' Percy put in. 'It seems to me, Doug, that if we do 'old back a bit so as not to upset your ma-in-law, we're entitled to some extra consideration. It seems to me that's only right and proper.'

'More interest, you mean?'

'That, too.'

'There's another aspect,' Ron said. 'We thought we were investing in the future. With old Wenning's death, the future's gone up the spout.'

'That's right,' Percy chimed in. 'A tame judge in the area in which we live could 'ave been a good investment. As I said just now, Doug, 'e didn't do us a favour by snuffing 'imself like that.'

Douglas had always been extremely dubious about any pressure that might profitably have been brought to bear on his father-in-law in his judicial capacity. But Ron and Percy Sugarman had been captivated by the thought, clearly believing themselves to be the first ever to have an English judge in their pocket. In his desire for the loan on behalf of his father-in-law, Douglas had made no attempt to disabuse them, nor, of course, had he warned Gerald Wenning of the risk he was running. After all, that was something he was able to work out for himself, for Douglas had told him that he would be obliged to go down some questionable byways in order to raise the money. The position had been that, so long as he could keep his own hands clean, Judge Wenning had been ready to accept money from any source and not enquire to deeply whence it came.

'I know you're not the only ones to have been thrown out by his death,' Douglas said.

'We're the only ones we're interested in,' Ron remarked in an uncompromising tone.

'And don't let's forget all the good turns we've done you, Doug,' Percy broke in. 'We've done things for you we wouldn't 'ave done for anyone else. You've been glad to 'ave us do your dirty work from time to time.'

'We've certainly always had a good working relationship,' Douglas said, squirming slightly in his chair. 'I've been grateful for your favours, just as I'm sure you've been grateful for mine.'

'That's true,' Percy said with a sigh. He turned to his brother. 'What shall we do, Ron, give it a bit longer to run before we decide anything?'

'Provided Doug realises it's up to him to see us right. Are you an executor of the old boy's will?'

'No. They're my mother-in-law and the family solicitor.'

'How's your wife come out of it?'

'She only benefits when her mother dies. Always supposing there's anything left when all the debts have been paid.'

'Well, don't let anyone forget that Mycroft Investments are holding out their hand.'

'That's right,' Percy added. 'Like some more coffee, Doug?'

'No, thanks.'

'What about another beer, Ron?'

'Nope.' After a pause he went on, 'Dolly was on the phone just before I came round. Ralphie Earle's been nicked.'

Percy Sugarman let out a low whistle. 'He's peterman for the Goodbody crowd,' he explained to Douglas. 'You know, an expert with the old geli. Or should I say gelignite to you Cotswold squires.'

Douglas smiled sourly. 'I'm well aware that a peterman is a safe-blower, but who are the Goodbody crowd? I've not heard of them.'

'That's your luck. They 'ang out in Acton. They're a real 'eavy mob. Ron and I keep out of their way.'

Douglas was relieved when, shortly afterwards, their

meeting broke up. It had not been as bad as he had expected, but that didn't mean he had any wish to prolong it.

There had been occasions when he thought he'd been fortunate to make the acquaintance of the Sugarmans. At other times, however, he regarded it as an ill day.

CHAPTER 14

It took Arthur a full day to recover from the shock of his afternoon at the police station. It was not so much the identification parade that had unnerved him as Chief Inspector Pennerly's belief that he was a murderer. There was bitter irony in the fact that, having successfully managed to evade prosecution over the past twenty-five years, he now stood in danger of being charged with a crime of which he was innocent and he was certainly in no mood to see it as poetic justice.

He realised that it would only be a matter of days at the most before Pennerly reappeared on his doorstep and he would need, when that moment arrived, to be able to point his own accusing finger in another direction.

There were, in his view, two obvious suspects, Greg and Judge Wenning. The police had apparently satisfied themselves that it wasn't Greg and it was a further irony that Arthur had given a fillip to that conclusion.

Greg had the motive all right, that of a jealous lover, but he also seemed to have had an alibi.

When he turned his thoughts to Judge Wenning, hope flickered more briefly. After all, who had had a stronger motive to murder Tony? He would obviously have assumed that the first blackmail letter came from him and only later on receipt of the second would he have concluded that Tony had a collaborator. Arthur wondered whether the police had already checked the judge's movements on the evening Tony was supposed to have been murdered. Probably they had, but surely the time of Tony's death was sufficiently imprecise to have allowed him opportunity as well as motive.

But, of course, the real advantage of casting suspicion on the judge was that he couldn't answer back. Arthur felt incensed when he reflected on the perverseness of the police in suspecting him.

Like a creature that only feels safe after dark, Arthur remained indoors until the street lights had come on and then went out to the shops. As he left the house, he noticed light in the basement flat and decided to pay a call on Greg on his return.

'Oh, hello,' Greg said, with a marked absence of enthusiasm when he opened the door. 'I was just doing a bit of packing.'

'May I come in for a few minutes?'

'If you don't mind the mess. And I'm afraid I can't offer you much; in fact, there's only only tea or coffee and I don't think there's any milk left.'

'I don't want anything, thank you,' Arthur said, stepping past him into the narrow passage. He took a few steps towards the kitchen before turning round abruptly and standing face to face with Greg. 'I want to have a serious word with you, Greg. What have you told the police about me?'

Greg swallowed uncomfortably and pushed past him into the kitchen. 'I've not told them anything,' he said.

'They suspect me of murdering Tony. You must have said something to them.'

'I haven't, Arthur, I promise you.'

'I wish I could believe that,' Arthur said sternly. 'I'm not saying that you've deliberately shopped me, but you must have told them something. What?'

'It's like I said the other day. I just told them how you and Tony were friendly and how you used to drop down here for a chat and a drink with them.' He frowned. 'They did seem keen to know whether I used to see you at your window as I came and went.'

'And what did you tell them?' Arthur enquired in a brittle tone.

'I told them you did seem to look out of the window quite a bit. But there's nothing wrong in that, is there?'

'Did they suggest I might have been spying on Tony's visitors?'

'In a sort of way. But I told them that, as I was out all day, I couldn't possibly know whether you did or not.'

'I see,' Arthur said grimly. 'If I may say so, Greg, I seem to have been a rather better friend to you than you've been to me.'

'That's not fair,' Greg said with a slight squirm. 'When the police have you for questioning, they spend the whole time twisting your answers and putting words into your mouth. Everyone knows that.'

A silence fell in an atmosphere which was heavy with reproach. It was broken by Arthur.

'Have the police, as far as you know, found anything here which might have suggested I was connected with Tony's death?'

'Definitely not, Arthur,' Greg said eagerly, as if anxious to make amends. 'Of course, I wasn't always here when they searched the place. They went over it several times, so they might have found something that gave them a false idea.'

'You don't think I killed Tony, do you?'

Greg looked at him in complete astonishment. 'How could you get such an idea, Arthur? Of course I don't. I mean, you had no reason to murder Tony. Even less than I had,' he added with a small tortured smile.

It was apparent that Greg knew nothing of Arthur's

blackmail attempt. He could only have learnt of it from the police and they had obviously kept their suspicions to themselves. Arthur wondered wryly whether he would have been given such a resounding vote of confidence had Greg been aware of the nature of the police allegation.

'But why on earth should they suspect you?' he now asked with a puzzled expression.

Arthur shook his head. 'It's a complete nightmare. All I can say is that they're terribly mistaken.'

'I'd have thought it was obvious to everyone that Tony was killed by a client. Probably one he'd never seen before in his life.' A tear trickled down Greg's cheek. 'Poor little Tony! How I miss him!'

On this somewhat melancholy note, Arthur took his leave and returned to his own flat two floors above.

The next day he ventured farther afield and ended up having lunch in the snack bar at Noone's. As he sat in the smoking room having a drink he recalled that his present troubles started there. It was too late to wish that he had never set eyes on Judge Wenning.

George Young came in, glancing about him and bestowing greetings on all and sundry. Noticing Arthur, he gave him a nod of recognition.

Probably thinks I'm just back from a secret mission, Arthur reflected sourly.

By the time he had finished his drink, the club's calm and civilised atmosphere had gone some way to restoring his sense of perspective. It was like being back in the womb.

After lunch he strolled along Piccadilly and up Bond Street. By the time he reached Oxford Street, however, he had had enough of crowded pavements. It was with a sense of relief that he caught a bus home.

He spent the rest of the afternoon and evening watching television and dwelling gloomily on the need to find a way of getting hold of some money.

This necessity was uppermost in his mind when he went to bed. He had once made a few hundred pounds by inserting an advertisement in a cranky religious journal appealing for funds (no individual subscription above £10 please) for the orphaned children of a devout sect in Ethiopia whose adult population had been heavily depleted by genocide.

It had been a gratifying response, as well as a reminder of the high degree of national gullibility always waiting to be exploited. Perhaps he should try and concoct another appeal on the same lines. Children or animals were always the best subject for such an approach to the public. It was with these thoughts in his mind that he fell asleep.

He had barely woken up the next morning when his door bell was given a vigorous ring. He glanced at his watch and saw that it wasn't yet eight o'clock. It could only be the postman with a parcel to deliver or the milkman wanting to remind him that he hadn't paid last week's bill.

He got out of bed and padded across to the window to peer out.

A police car was parked at the kerb.

'Yes?' he said nervously into the intercom.

'It's Chief Inspector Pennerly, Mr Kedby. Press your buzzer. I want to come up and see you.' A few seconds later, Pennerly appeared on the landing and greeted Arthur who was standing in the open doorway looking alarmed. 'I like your dressing-gown,' he said with a glimmer of a smile. 'Sorry if I've got you out of bed, but I wanted to be certain of finding you at home.' He produced a piece of paper from his pocket and dangled it in front of Arthur's face. 'It's a search warrant obtained under the Theft Act, Mr Kedby,' he said, pushing past Arthur into the flat. 'Don't shut the door, Detective Sergeant Allen will be here in a moment.'

'I don't understand,' Arthur said when speech returned to him. 'Did you say a search warrant under the Theft

Act? I've not stolen anything. What is it you're looking for?'

At that moment Terry Allen arrived.

'Let's start with these drawers,' Pennerly said to him, moving across to a cabinet in which Arthur kept assorted items.

'I demand to know what you're looking for,' he said, with a spurt of anger. It was intolerable to stand in his own room and be ignored.

He watched them make a methodical search through the drawers of the cabinet, tidily replacing every item before turning to the next.

'You'd better not try and plant anything on me,' he shouted at them.

'Don't worry, Mr Kedby, we shan't,' Pennerly remarked. 'I'm not interested in framing you on a minor drugs charge or for handling a stolen watch, if that's what's bothering you. I'm going to have you on a murder charge or nothing!'

Arthur felt suddenly weak at the knees and sat down. It was as if he had been abandoned to a ghastly fate. Here were these two ordinary-looking young men treating him with perfect civility, but with only one thing in their minds, namely to find evidence on which they could charge him with murder.

As he watched them going about their task, he felt the blood drain from his face and he began to tremble for it had just dawned on him what they could be looking for. And if not actually looking for, what they might find.

He sat mesmerised as they came closer to the drawer in which the object lay hidden beneath a pile of old magazines.

'Getting warmer, are we?' Pennerly said over his shoulder when he noticed Arthur's expression.

'I don't know what you mean. I still have no idea what you're searching for.'

'That's not what your expression says,' Pennerly said

pleasantly. 'You ought to take a look at yourself in the mirror. You're a picture of acute alarm.'

Arthur closed his eyes. Any moment now they were going to find it and he didn't want to see. He heard the bottom drawer being opened (it had its own particular squeak) and held his breath.

'Take a look at this, sir,' Allen said in a satisfied tone.

'You can open your eyes, Mr Kedby,' Pennerly remarked. 'We've found what we were hopefully looking for.'

Arthur opened his eyes as if coming out of a trance.

'Perhaps you'll tell us how you come to have this,' he went on, holding up John Smith's Australian passport.

'I found it,' Arthur said in a sort of croak.

'Where?'

'On the pavement outside a pub in Earls Court Road.'

'When?'

'I can't remember.'

'When?'

'It could have been two or three weeks ago. I really don't remember.'

'And you brought it home?'

'I was intending to hand it in next time I was near the police station.'

'And why didn't you?'

'I put it away in that drawer for safe-keeping and it completely slipped my mind.'

'If you could hear yourself, Mr Kedby, you'd realise how implausible that sounds.'

'It's the truth.'

'I doubt it. But tell me this, have you put it to any use since finding it?'

Arthur shook his head vehemently. 'I assure you, I haven't been abroad this year.'

'There are other ways of using passports,' Pennerly said mildly. 'For example to prove identity. Supposing Mr

John Smith wanted to collect the mail waiting for him at Trafalgar Square Post Office, he'd need to take along some document to prove who he was.' He paused and gave Arthur a thoughtful stare. 'I think you'd better get dressed and accompany us back to the police station. We'll want you to take part in another identification parade. There's a young post office clerk who believes he might be able to recognise Mr John Smith again. Be as well to bring your toothbrush and shaving tackle with you.'

Arthur felt the room spin and toppled sideways off his chair.

His flight from reality was, however, brief, lasting only until Sergeant Allen dashed some cold water into his face. The two officers helped him to his feet and supported him across to the bed.

'Just sit down for a couple of minutes and you'll be perfectly all right,' Pennerly said. 'Have you got any brandy?'

Arthur shook his head slowly. 'I don't want any brandy. I'd like a cup of tea.'

Pennerly sighed and nodded to Terry Allen who walked over to the stove and picked up the kettle.

'It'll have to be a quick one as I want to get back to the station. Meanwhile, you can get dressed and pack your overnight bag. You won't be returning here for a while.'

The day that had begun so dramatically for Arthur ended for him in Brixton prison where he was to spend the next five months awaiting his trial at the Old Bailey.

CHAPTER 15

Arthur was later to look back on the day of his arrest rather as a tin of corned beef might look back on the day it went to the slaughterhouse as a young bullock.

There was the identification parade at which the post office clerk first failed to identify anyone, but then on a return along the line picked out Arthur, adding audibly to the officer in charge that he wasn't absolutely sure.

After that, Arthur had been charged and taken to court where he made a two-minute appearance before being granted legal aid and remanded in custody for seven days.

Finally there had been the claustrophobic ride in the prison van and the arrival at Brixton prison where a further conveyor belt awaited him. A day of activity interspersed with long periods of tedium waiting for the next thing to happen. A day in which he had been required to do nothing save stand and sit at other people's dictation.

Six days later he was fetched from his cell to receive a visit from his solicitor. He had been given a piece of paper which informed him that a firm named Snaith and Epton had been assigned to his defence. He had not, however, been expecting to meet anyone from the firm until he was back in court the next day. His cell mate, who held a poor view of the entire legal profession, had told him he would be lucky to receive as much attention as a new recruit might expect from an army barber.

'It's the same with the doctors and dentists these days,' his companion had added with gloomy relish. 'You're no more than a form and a national insurance number.'

Arthur stopped in his tracks as he entered the interview cubicle, for sitting waiting for him was a small, almost elflike girl. She glanced up from the pad of paper on which she was writing and looked at him with large brown eyes.

'I'm Rosa Epton of Snaith and Epton,' she said. 'Why don't you sit down, Mr Kedby? My firm holds the legal aid certificate in your case. I always like to meet my clients as soon as possible after they've been charged. As you'll observe,' she went on, gesturing at the glass partition at the farther side of which prison officers moved around in a central area, 'we can be seen but not heard.'

'You're my solicitor?' Arthur said, wondering how anyone who looked so appealing and vulnerable could have descended into the murky realm of criminal practice.

'Yes. Do you have any objection?'

'Oh, no. None at all.'

'That's all right then,' she said briskly. 'Though you can always apply to the court for a change of solicitor if you become dissatisfied with the way I'm handling your defence.' She gave him a faint smile. 'And, of course, I can do likewise if I don't think we're getting on. But I'm sure that won't happen.' She put up her hands and brushed back her hair which had a tendency to fall forward on either side of her face. 'Right, let's begin. First I'd like to hear the whole story from your point of view. Remember, all I've heard so far are one or two lines from the police. Later on, the crown will be serving witnesses' statements on us, but meanwhile I'd like to hear your version of events.' She picked up her pen and smoothed the sheet of paper in front of her. 'I'll be making some notes, but take no notice of me and just go on talking. I'm trained to write and listen at the same time.'

Arthur had realised by this time that Rosa Epton had a far more robust spirit than her looks suggested. He noticed that when she wrote, her tongue peeped out from the corner of her mouth, like that of a child concentrating on drawing a picture.

'So you didn't make a written statement under caution?' she said when he reached the end.

'No.'

'That makes a nice change,' she observed, pushing her hair back from her face again.

Arthur felt unable to tell her that, though this was his first direct confrontation with the law, he was by no means an innocent in what went on.

'And you have no previous convictions of any sort?'

'None.'

'Good,' she said in a satisfied tone. 'Well, there's not much more I can do until we receive the bundle of statements from the D.P.P. We'll almost certainly agree to a section one committal. That means, no evidence called at the magistrates' court. I'm afraid, however, it's likely to be several months before your case comes up at the Old Bailey. But I'll see you at court each week between now and the committal for trial and we'll need to have a long conference when we've both studied the crown's evidence.'

She thrust her pad of paper into her briefcase and rose. She was wearing a black chunky sweater with a high loose collar and a pair of burgundy red slacks.

'Thank you very much for coming,' Arthur said. 'I really appreciate your visit.'

She raised an eyebrow in mild surprise. 'It's all part of my job, Mr Kedby. I'll see you at court tomorrow morning.'

She turned and left the cubicle and a prison officer

entered to escort Arthur back to his cell block. He felt as if the sun had gone in.

When Rosa Epton arrived back at her office, she poked her head round her partner's door.

'Hi! Come on in and tell me how Brixton was looking today,' Robin Snaith said, removing his spectacles and leaning back relaxedly in his desk chair.

He was around forty and had been a one-man firm specialising in criminal defence work when Rosa had joined him as a clerk. She had quickly established herself as his indispenable assistant and he had had no hesitation in encouraging her to become qualified. He had then lost no time in offering her a partnership with the firm's name being changed to include hers. He had realised that she wanted to remain with him and suspected that she would have done so even if he had offered her less attractive terms. But even the remote prospect of losing such an efficient and intuitively shrewd assistant was not to be contemplated.

The firm was highly regarded and its success lay not merely in its partners being conscientious and good at their jobs, but in their ability to avoid the snares involved in representing ruthless and self-interested criminals. Robin Snaith could exhibit his own brand of ruthlessness in protecting his professional integrity and Rosa, despite all appearances, was in no way his inferior in this respect.

'As far as I'm concerned, Brixton prison is about as exhilarating as an old grey blanket. I really hate the place. I think it's the mixture of flickering hope and bleak despair that gets me down. I suppose it's inevitable to find that in a remand prison.'

'You've always been sensitive to atmosphere, haven't you?' Robin remarked.

Rosa smiled. 'Don't worry, I'm not about to go into a decline.'

'What I really meant by my question, of course, was how did you find our client?'

'I'm not sure about him,' she said pensively. 'He's an innocuous-looking little man, very polite and well spoken, but...'

'But what?'

'I don't think I'd trust him very far. To be quite frank, I find it much easier to envisage him as a blackmailer than as a murderer.'

'I gather the police see him as both.'

'But he's only been charged with murder. I know they suspect him of blackmail because Pennerly told me as much. But they lack evidence.'

'How strong is the murder charge?'

'From what Kedby says, the evidence is purely circumstantial, but, of course, I've not yet seen the statements. They may present a somewhat different picture from the one he gave me.'

'What's the broad outline of the police allegation?'

'That the dead man, Ching, and our client blackmailed Judge Wenning. And that the two blackmailers fell out over a division of the spoils, which led to Kedby murdering Ching.'

'Quite a bit of supposition in all that, I'd say. Is there any evidence, for example, that Wenning ever paid over any money?'

'Not that I'm aware of. Pennerly was rather cagey on the phone and obviously not disposed to discuss the case in any detail. But if Wenning did pay up and the police had evidence of the fact, I'd have expected a charge of blackmail to have been preferred.'

'So would I. The fact that it hasn't seems to point to the contrary. In which event, there weren't any spoils to divide, so what was our client's motive for murdering Ching?'

Rosa nodded. 'I know. It all sounds pretty tenuous, but

it's no good pre-judging anything at this stage. We'll have to wait until the statements have been served on us.' She paused and then said, 'What can you tell me about Judge Wenning, Robin?'

'I came across him a few times when he was in practice, but I never briefed him. He just wasn't my type. He was slightly pompous and I always regarded him as something of a bully. He was inclined to harass witnesses and obviously rather enjoyed doing so.'

'What was he like as a judge?'

'Quite good, I believe. At any rate, the police liked him.'

'That's not necessarily a recommendation.'

Robin laughed. 'When I say "liked", I don't mean that he was popular, because I gather he wasn't. But he was a tough judge, particularly with young vandals and hooligans which met with police approval. Indeed, mine, too.'

'Do you know anything about his personal life?'

'Nothing to his discredit. I'd certainly never heard a whisper to suggest he was homosexually inclined. He'd either suppressed it until latterly or else been exceedingly discreet.'

'But it doesn't surprise you?'

Robin glanced at her in mild astonishment. 'I can't remember when I was last surprised by something of that nature. You know what they say about homosexual conduct. Half the population doesn't believe it goes on, and the other half practises it. I suppose there's a third category made up of the police and legal profession, the great majority of whom don't practise it, but who are very much aware that it goes on.'

'That's true,' Rosa said with a little sigh. 'Anyway, it looks like an interesting case and one with a run for the defence. I get so bored with cases which are completely sewn up before they ever get to us.' She reached for her briefcase and stood up. 'I'd better get back to my room and see what else awaits.'

She and Robin had always had the habit of dropping in on each other on their return from court or visiting clients in prison. If either was particularly busy, a sign was all that was needed to send the other on his way.

Robin watched her go through the door with an expression of respect and affection. Her one weakness was a slight tendency to fall for some of her younger clients. Even though she always managed to keep her feelings well under control, he was able to tell when it had happened.

At least there seemed no danger of it happening in the case of Arthur Kedby.

CHAPTER 16

For Arthur the next six weeks dragged by with agonising slowness, the dreary routine of prison existence being broken only by his weekly visit to court in order to be remanded in custody for a further seven days.

He would see Rosa Epton briefly on these occasions, her visits to him in the cells being more dutiful than for any practical purpose.

'I'm afraid there's nothing to be done until the prosecution has served the statements on us,' she would say each time he asked how much longer he was going to be transported back and forth without anything happening.

He gained a crumb of comfort when she began chivvying Chief Inspector Pennerly on his excursions into the witness-box to seek a further remand in custody.

'How many more times are you going to be making this application?' she asked him crisply on Arthur's fourth appearance at court.

Pennerly looked pained. 'We still have a number of enquiries to make,' he said, hoping for a sign of sympathy from the magistrate, but receiving none.

'You obviously considered you had enough evidence when you charged my client four weeks ago, so why this delay?'

'I assure you we're not wasting time,' he said stiffly.

Rosa turned to the magistrate. 'I urge you, sir, to give the police and the D.P.P. a time limit to present their case. I'm not accusing Mr Pennerly of dragging his feet, but I sometimes think the police would do well to reflect on the demoralising effect this kind of week by week custody can have on somebody who has not previously faced it. It's a particularly cruel form of limbo . . .'

'Yes, thank you, Miss Epton,' the magistrate broke in hastily. 'I certainly have no intention of acceding to indefinite requests for further remands and I'm sure that Detective Chief Inspector Pennerly will convey what I have said to his superiors and to the Director of Public Prosecutions.'

A few minutes later when he met Rosa outside the court, Pennerly said, 'That was hitting a bit below the belt. You know it's not my fault.'

'I thought I made that clear,' Rosa said. 'But I really do feel strongly about these endless remands in custody. They're not fair.'

'It's the system. It's overloaded.'

'I know. That's why it's necessary to make a song and dance at every opportunity. It's the only way to get things changed.'

'Some hope!'

'*I*'ve not yet become a resigned cynic,' she said in a challenging tone.

'I hope I'm not one either.'

'Too many people in our respective jobs are.'

'Probably. But, if I may say so, Miss Epton, you can't expect all your geese to turn out as swans.'

Rosa sighed. If Pennerly chose to believe she so regarded her client, that was his concern.

'Just as I suppose you'd never admit that the police have sometimes charged an innocent person,' she said with a touch of needle.

He looked at her with his head cocked on one side. 'But

not in this case, Miss Epton. If the jury acquit Kedby, it'll be for want of evidence, not on account of his innocence.'

They smiled at each other with the wariness of two contestants in a beauty competition.

Rosa, in fact, regarded Pennerly rather more highly than she did many of his colleagues. For a start, she believed him to be straight, though that didn't mean he would be above snatching a quick trick if he saw the opportunity; for example, in his careful blandishments to a suspect to make a statement, which would subsequently hang round his neck like a millstone.

It was not too long after this encounter with Pennerly that she received the bundle of statements on which the prosecution were relying to prove the charge of murder. She immediately sent a set off to Brixton prison with a message to Arthur that she would visit him there the next day to go through them with him.

Arthur received the statements as if they were a surprise birthday present.

The following afternoon he was escorted from his cell across to the interview centre and to the room in which one awaited the arrival of one's solicitor in the block. He hugged the bundle of statements to his chest. It wasn't long before he was led to one of the glass-sided interview cubicles where Rosa was already sitting. He observed that on this occasion she had reversed her colours and was wearing black slacks and a burgundy red polo-neck sweater. A large pear-shaped ruby-coloured stone dangled from a gold chain round her neck.

'No need to ask if you've read the statements,' she said with a small smile as he sat down. 'I can see that from the notes in the margins. Let's go through them from the beginning and you tell me the bits with which you disagree.'

'These people – the woman and the two boys – who say

that they saw me in Gerrards Cross are lying. How could they have seen me when I wasn't there?'

'But they all picked you out on the identification parade.'

'They're mistaken.'

'The trouble is that you were allegedly seen on two separate occasions. The woman mentions one day and the boys another over a week later. Moreover, you've admitted hiring a car and driving in the vicinity of Gerrards Cross on what is now proved to be the day the woman says she saw you.'

Arthur gave a helpless shrug. 'It must have been my double they saw. As I told the police, I drove through the place, but I never stopped. And I certainly didn't stare over anyone's garden fence.'

'I'm afraid juries don't go much for doubles who pop up and land innocent people in trouble,' Rosa said crisply.

'But what else am I to think?' Arthur wailed. 'And, after all, I'm a fairly ordinary-looking person. I look quite anonymous in a crowd. I have no memorable features.'

'If you weren't there, you weren't there,' Rosa said briskly, 'but I must point out that if the jury happen to believe those witnesses, you could be sunk.'

Not as sunk as if I tell the truth, Arthur reflected grimly.

'If it were just the woman alone or the two boys on their own it wouldn't be so difficult to explain away, but it's their combined effect. I suppose you have no witnesses to say you were elsewhere on those two occasions?'

Arthur shook his head. 'Can you . . .?'

'Can I what, Mr Kedby?' she asked severely.

'Nothing.'

'Good. My firm doesn't provide that sort of service, if that's what you were wondering.' Having delivered her reproof, she turned back to the statements. 'What about Ching's flat-mate, Greg French? Anything in his statement with which you disagree?'

'Nothing specific, but his main concern was to save his own skin. He was quite prepared to cast blame on me if it was going to help *him*.'

'His statement strikes me as being fairly harmless.'

'Except that he makes out that I was constantly in their flat visiting Tony, which isn't true. And how would he know anyway, seeing that he was at work all day?'

'I think you're taking a more pessimistic view of his statement than is called for. He's saying no more than that you and Ching were on neighbourly terms. He's certainly not suggesting that you had any motive for murdering him.'

'That would be a diabolical liberty.'

'Now, what about John Smith's passport?' Rosa went on in a businesslike tone.

'It's just as I explained to Chief Inspector Pennerly. I found it and meant to hand it in at a police station, but put it in a drawer and forgot all about it.'

'That was an unfortunate oversight. Forgetting to hand it in, I mean.'

'I realise that now.'

'You'll almost certainly be asked by someone how it came to be at the bottom of a drawer beneath other things. It'd be as well to have an answer ready.' She met Arthur's wooden gaze and went on, 'What about the post office clerk who picked you out as the person asking for mail in the name of John Smith?'

'It wasn't a proper identification,' Arthur expostulated, glad to be on what he regarded as firmer ground. 'He stood there dithering and suddenly pointed in my direction. I believe an officer made a signal to him.'

'You're not suggesting that the officer in charge of the parade . . .'

'No, not him,' Arthur broke in. 'But we were standing with our backs to some windows and it would have been easy for someone to have indicated me.'

'Do you seriously believe that happened?' Rosa asked, with a touch of scorn.

'It could have done,' Arthur said without great conviction.

'But if it didn't, it means you have been picked out a fourth time on an identification parade. I agree he doesn't appear to have made an entirely spontaneous identification, but he did make one after hesitation.' She turned over another page of the statements in front of her. 'You've read what the handwriting expert says? It's on page twelve.'

'Yes.'

'That the two envelopes found in Judge Wenning's possession could have been addressed by the same person (namely, you) who gave a sample of writing to the police.'

'All he says is *could have been,*' Arthur said, with his own touch of scorn. 'He doesn't say that I did write them.'

'Handwriting experts are rarely as positive as that,' Rosa observed drily. 'Anyway, your answer is that it wasn't you who addressed the envelopes to Judge Wenning.'

'I didn't even know him. I'd never heard of him until I read of his death. Why should I have written to him?'

'Don't waste your rhetoric on me, Mr Kedby!' Rosa said with a quick smile.

'But I'm not sure that you believe me,' he said in a reproachful voice.

'It doesn't matter whether I believe or disbelieve you,' she replied, giving him a long, steady look. 'My job is to find out your answers to points made by the prosecution witnesses and in doing so, I'm bound to ask you a number of supplementary questions.'

'I'm sorry, I didn't mean to sound critical.'

'That's all right. Most clients want to be believed. It's natural. In the final event, however, the only people who matter are the twelve jurors.'

It was a further half-hour before Rosa began to put

her papers back into her briefcase. Arthur watched her with a worried expression.

'What do you think my chances are?' he asked nervously.

'I'm sorry, but I never answer that question. But don't look so downcast. The crown's case has gaps in it and we'll certainly do our best to widen them. I'll see you at court the day after tomorrow, when you'll be committed for trial. After that, I'll be briefing counsel and then we'll just have to wait for the case to be listed.'

When he got back to his cell, Arthur lay down on his bed and reviewed his situation. He realised that the case against him might be worse, but he was in no mood to be grateful for mercies, large or small. He was filled with a mixture of frustration and self-pity.

'I'm more than ever certain they've charged him with the wrong offence,' Rosa said to Robin Snaith when she returned to her office. 'I'm positive he was blackmailing Wenning, but the police can't charge him because no blackmail demands have ever been found and Judge Wenning in his farewell note referred only to his life being in a mess, which could mean anything. They're going to hint at blackmail, of course, because it's their only way of suggesting a motive.'

'From what you've told me about the case,' Robin said, 'the crown is on weak ground for a number of reasons. First, they're unable to *prove* that Wenning ever visited Tony Ching. Having his telephone number isn't proof of a visit. Secondly, they can't *prove* that blackmail was ever attempted. Thirdly, they can't *prove* that Kedby and Ching were collaborators. Fourthly, without evidence of blackmail, they're unable to advance any sort of motive against our client. And, finally, they're forced to accept that murder is always an occupational hazard for anyone in Ching's trade.'

'Put like that, Kedby should walk out,' Rosa said with

a sigh. 'The trouble is that he's not going to be a very convincing witness on his own behalf.'

'Hmm. Whom are you thinking of briefing?'

'I haven't decided.'

'It may be one of those cases for keeping the defendant out of the witness-box.'

'That's always a risky thing to do.'

'Sometimes it's a risk worth taking. Counsel can tear up as much of the prosecution evidence as he can in cross-examination and then make a powerful submission of no case to answer. Even if the judge overrules it, it doesn't follow that the jury will convict despite no evidence being called on behalf of the defence. After all, there's a different standard of proof to be satisfied at each stage.'

'I think that sounds like a good idea, Robin. I'll certainly canvass it with counsel.' She gave her senior partner a pleased smile. 'Personally, I believe Pennerly jumped the gun. If he'd consulted the D.P.P. before charging Kedby with murder, I suspect he'd have been advised to look around for more evidence. Now, of course, the D.P.P. and Treasury counsel are landed with the case and will have to make the best of it they can.' She paused and added wryly, 'The further I'm away from Arthur Kedby, the weaker seems to be the case against him.'

CHAPTER 17

Since her husband's death, Diana Wenning had managed to close her mind to him, except when she was absolutely obliged to give him thought. It didn't upset her when she had to do this, but as soon as the reason for calling him to mind had been dealt with, she once more closed the door on his memory.

The house at Gerrards Cross had been quickly sold for a substantial price and with what was left of the proceeds, she had bought a small flat in one of the less fashionable Kensington streets.

She had asked her son-in-law to handle all the business details arising from her husband's demise, making it clear that she had no wish to be bothered unless necessary. In the circumstances, this had suited Douglas very well and he had been able to pay off his father-in-law's creditors (including himself) without having to enter upon any awkward explanations. This applied particularly in the case of Ron and Percy Sugarman whose loans, channelled through himself, had remained *sub rosa*.

Christine had suggested that her mother should move nearer to them and had been taken aback by her decision to buy a flat in London.

'I intend to catch up on life,' Diana told everyone. 'I

was becoming too much of a recluse in the country, anyway.'

As rumours of Gerald Wenning's conduct had circulated, friends had rallied to her side with moral support only to discover that it wasn't needed. She wouldn't actually rebuff them while they were making their sympathetic noises, but would wait until they had finished and then change the subject.

About two weeks before Arthur's trial was due to open, Christine drove up to London to spend the day with her mother. They had lunch at a small Italian restaurant and returned afterwards to the flat.

'That man's trial comes up at the Old Bailey soon,' Christine said as they sat down.

'Oh, really. I didn't know,' her mother replied vaguely.

'Douglas thinks the family ought to be represented by counsel. It's called a watching brief.'

'I don't see any need myself, but if Douglas likes to do something about it, it's up to him.'

'It could be a very testing time for all of us.'

'In what way, dear?'

'You'll have the media on the phone and knocking at the door.'

'It's extraordinary the way that word has slipped into everyday usage. Nobody talked about the media ten years ago. Anyway, I shall refuse to speak to any of them.'

'You do realise, don't you, that reference is bound to be made to Daddy's association with that Chinese boy?'

'I hadn't really thought about it.' She frowned. 'Remind me again of the name of the man on trial. I know it's something like Cadbury.'

'It's Kedby. Arthur Kedby. You know that Mrs Barker is going to be a witness.'

'How could I forget! She was so full of importance after she reported having seen a man staring through our fence. And being asked to attend an identification parade was an accolade in itself. She'll love being a witness at the Old Bailey. Thank goodness we're no longer next door neighbours.'

'Well, as long as you're forewarned,' Christine said, with a small exasperated sigh.

'I wish now I'd bought that curtain material we saw in the window on our way back from lunch. I've a good mind to go back to the shop later on.' Observing her daughter's expression, she said, 'What's worrying you, dear?'

'To be absolutely frank, Mummy, you are. You don't seem to be alive to all the muck that's likely to be raked over in the course of the trial.'

'I'm perfectly alive to it, but there's nothing I can do to prevent it and so I don't let my mind dwell on it.'

'Aren't you upset at the prospect of Daddy's name being bandied about in such a sordid context?'

'Naturally, I would sooner it wasn't, but I have no feelings of responsibility whatsoever in the matter.'

'It seems to me you're deliberately sticking your head in the sand.'

'Perhaps I am. But if people expect me to appear a figure of humiliation, I'm afraid they're in for a disappointment. I decline to feel humiliated. It now turns out that your father treated me abominably, but I have no wish to dwell on that fact. It's an era of my life that's over and done with. He brought disgrace on his own unhappy head. I'd never placed him on a pedestal and I now feel quite detached about his behaviour.' She glanced at her watch. 'I think I will go back to that shop where we saw the curtain material. Are you coming with me?'

Christine, however, bade her mother a terse farewell and set off for home in her car.

She arrived to find her husband watching television with his feet up and a large whisky in his hand.

'I think the shock's done something to Mummy's mind,'

she said as she flopped down on to the sofa beside him. 'Her whole attitude is most peculiar.'

Douglas listened in dour silence while she related the details of her visit.

'I still think we ought to have counsel with a watching brief,' he said, getting up to fetch himself another drink. 'Your mother's always behaved a bit oddly at times.'

'She's not against the idea. She left it entirely to you.'

'I mean, supposing the defence start suggesting to the jury that it could have been your father who murdered Ching. It's always easy to smear the dead, they can't answer back, but at least we must know what's being said.'

'But what could we do?'

'If that suggestion *is* made and if Kedby gets off, we could later issue a statement to the press.'

'Repudiating the slur?'

'Something of that sort.'

'Not that it'll bother Mummy in her present mood if it *is* suggested that her husband was a murderer in addition to everything else.'

'Your mother's not the only person concerned,' Douglas said flatly. 'I'll probably try and attend a bit of the trial myself. You can look after the shop for a couple of days, can't you?'

Christine gave him an anxious look. 'Do you think that's a good idea? Wouldn't it be better if we all kept right away? After all, if we have counsel with a watching brief, there's no need for either of us to attend.'

'I've already asked that young sergeant to let me know when the case is due to start,' he said in a tone that was intended to settle the matter.

'You didn't tell me.'

'I've told you now.' After a pause, he added, 'From what you say, it's as well your mother isn't required as a witness.'

'I don't know why she isn't.'

'I gather it's because your father's suicide isn't a main issue in the murder trial and, in any event, it can be proved by the police witnesses.'

Christine got up. 'I suppose I had better go and prepare supper.' She sniffed the air. 'Who's been smoking a cigar in here?'

'Percy Sugarman.'

'You didn't tell me he was coming.'

'He phoned after you'd left.'

'What was the object of his visit?'

'He wanted to show me one or two things.'

'Anything worth buying?'

'There was a Queen Anne coffee pot, but he wanted too much for it.'

'I can't help wondering where he and his brother get hold of some of their stuff. I hope they'll never land you in any trouble.'

Douglas shook his head dismissively.

'They've been good friends. Your father certainly had much to thank them for.'

'I wish you'd never told me that you borrowed money from them to lend to Daddy. I hate to think of his having been beholden to men like that.'

'Your father wasn't fussy where the money came from.'

'I seem to be the only person who remembers him with any affection,' she said in a sad voice.

Her husband tactfully refrained from agreeing.

'By the way, Percy Sugarman sent you his love. He likes you even if you don't like him. But you won't be seeing him for some time. He's off to his villa in Spain for a couple of months in ten days' time.'

CHAPTER 18

Five days before Arthur's trial began, Rosa drove down to Brixton prison with Piers Brendon, the junior of the two counsel she had briefed for the defence.

He was a plump, jolly man in his late thirties, who had a way with juries and who never panicked. He was given to wearing a bowler hat tilted back on his head which accentuated his general impression of roundness.

Rosa frequently briefed him and felt he was somewhat wasted when, as in this case, he had a leader. Mr Francis Radley, Q.C., whom she had also briefed was unable to make the visit to Brixton.

Arthur had found the long wait between committal and trial hard to bear. There hadn't even been the weekly excursion to the magistrates' court to break the routine and Rosa had been to see him only twice. At times he was engulfed by waves of self-pity and felt he had been abandoned.

'This is Mr Brendon, who will be defending you,' she said when Arthur was shown into the interview cubicle.

'That's right,' Brendon said cheerfully. 'Sorry Mr Radley couldn't manage to come with us today, but I expect we'll get by without him. He's leading for the defence, as I'm sure Miss Epton has told you.' He slipped the noose of pink tape from his brief and flattened down the papers with two chubby hands. 'Not very much to ask you actually, because, as usual, Miss Epton has covered everything in her excellent instructions.' He beamed at Rosa who modestly kept her eyes fixed on her own set of papers. 'I think you've seen the notice of additional evidence the prosecution has served on us.'

Arthur nodded. 'I suppose they're allowed to do that?'

Piers Brendon let out a gusty laugh. 'Allowed to? I've known cases where they've rained down like confetti even after a trial has started, but judges can get a bit shirty when that happens. Let's see what this further witness says. Name's Herbert Foreman. Says he was on duty at the car park in Uxbridge the day you hired a car from Jolly's in Gloucester Road. He'll testify that a car bearing the registration number of the one you hired was left in the car park that morning. He goes on to say that they don't normally record them, but because of recent troubles in the running of the car park, a check of every car using it was made on that particular day. It was one of several spot checks made over a period of a month.' He gave Arthur a comical smile. 'I take it you're not denying that you parked there?'

Arthur shook his head sullenly in a way that indicated he would certainly have done so if it had been feasible.

'So the real question is why?'

'I wanted to buy some bits and pieces for a picnic lunch.'

'Sounds most reasonable, but I suppose some nasty person may ask, why Uxbridge?'

'Because I happened to notice shops and somewhere to park at the same moment.'

'A happy coincidence, indeed, in these days when one can spend longer looking for somewhere to park than getting to one's destination. Was there any reason why you didn't mention this break in your journey when the police were quizzing you?'

'It never occurred to me. All they seemed interested in was whether I stopped in Gerrards Cross.'

'I follow. Did you happen to know that Judge Wenning sat in a court at Uxbridge?'

'At that time, I'd never even heard of Judge Wenning.' Arthur had told this particular lie so many times that it tripped effortlessly off his tongue.

'Well that seems to clear up that little matter. Coming to something quite different, how do you feel about going into the witness-box and giving evidence?'

Arthur grimaced. 'It's bound to be an ordeal. I know how easily one's words can be twisted and taken out of context.'

Brendon let out a merry laugh. 'Oh, dear, our reputation at the Bar sinks with each new television court-room drama.' Suddenly serious again, he asked, 'Would you mind if you didn't give evidence?'

Arthur blinked in surprise. 'But surely the jury'll immediately think I'm guilty if I don't.'

'The crown has to prove its case beyond a reasonable doubt. If its evidence falls short, it isn't incumbent on a defendant to make any defence. The prosecution has failed and that's that. Anyway, I wanted to sound you out, because it may be that when the time comes our advice to you will be not to go into the witness-box. Should that be our advice, you're still not obliged to take it. In a matter of that nature, the final decision has to be yours.' He shuffled his papers together. 'Is there anything you want to ask me, Mr Kedby, for the next time we meet will be at the Old Bailey?'

'Will you be suggesting who might have done the murder?'

'Our job is to persuade the jury that you didn't. We don't have to advance alternative candidates.'

'But don't you think it could have been Judge Wenning himself?'

'Possibly. Or it could have been any of the other ships that passed in the night. We shall certainly be impressing on the jury what a dangerous trade Ching was engaged in.'

'Who'll be the judge?' Arthur asked anxiously as Brendon reached for his bowler and put it on at its usual insouciant angle.

'Probably Mr Justice Michaelson.'

'What's he like?'

Brendon gave another merry laugh. 'A bit slow and fussy and conscience-ridden. He was destined for the church, but made a U-turn and landed in the law instead. He's a brilliant lawyer, but not at his happiest trying criminal cases.'

Later during their drive back into central London, he said to Rosa, 'I'm afraid this whole case is going to cause old Michaelson acute anguish. Male prostitution and a judge who's behaved scandalously! But it'll do him good to be reminded that sin knows no social confines.'

'He looks so desiccated.'

'He's more desiccated than a packet of that coconut.' After a pause Brendon added, 'But I can't help feeling a bit sorry for him when he's trying crime. He so obviously regards it as a sentence of purgatory.'

A little later, Rosa said, 'What was your impression of our client?'

'Moderately unattractive. But I agree with you that he looks much more like a blackmailer than a murderer. And if he had murdered Ching, I don't believe he would have strangled him with a belt. There was something particularly cruel and nasty about that. Much more the act of a sadist. It's another point we must rub into the jury.' He was thoughtful for a moment, 'Now, Gerald Wenning *would* have been capable of it.'

CHAPTER 19

Arthur woke even earlier than usual on the morning of his trial. It was quite dark outside the high window of his cell and he lay beneath his coarse blanket in uneasy contemplation of the day ahead. It was, he felt, like setting out on a hazardous journey to one of the world's danger spots. Survival was by no means assured, but hope was essential.

He put on a clean shirt and his best suit which Rosa had collected from his flat and sent to him for the occasion. She had told him that she had personally selected the tie to go with the shirt. It was dark blue with large silver spots. Her action had been one of several she had conceived to boost his morale during the long wait.

After breakfast he and about twenty others destined for the Old Bailey that day were herded together to await the arrival of the prison vans which would convey them to court.

Arthur found himself standing beside a short foxy-looking man with a pasty complexion and a head of thinning ginger hair. He had noticed him on a number of occasions during exercise, but had never had any conversation with him.

'You're up for murder, aren't you?' his companion said, looking at Arthur with interest.

'Yes, but I didn't do it.'

' 'Course you didn't. Got any form 'ave you?'

'No.'

'Not that it'd make any difference in your case. It's life or nothing for you.'

'What are you charged with?' Arthur enquired.

His companion gave him a look of sharp surprise. 'Don't you know who I am?'

'I'm afraid not.'

'Ralphie Earle, that's who I am. They've got me on conspiracy to rob. It's a bloody liberty, too.'

'Does that mean you have a co-defendant?'

'He's scarpered, which is another bloody liberty. I 'ardly knew the bloke. We never conspired to do nothing.'

'Are you hoping to get off?'

' 'Course I'm 'oping, but it won't be thanks to any bloody coppers. Corrupt lot of bastards! They've been after me since I came out last time. Talk about bloody persecution!' He gave Arthur a sly wink. 'Luckily, I've got friends . . .'

At that point their conversation ended as a senior prison officer shouted for silence. Shortly afterwards they were escorted to the waiting prison vans.

On arrival at the Old Bailey they were escorted to the custody area and locked in separate cells. There was over an hour to go before the courts were due to sit. To Arthur's surprise he was offered a cup of tea.

'But don't go holding up your hand as soon as you get into court,' the officer who gave it to him said. 'Wasn't it Napoleon or somebody who said, pee when you can or you mayn't get another opportunity? That applies here.'

Soon after ten o'clock, Rosa appeared in his cell accompanied by his two counsel.

Francis Radley, Q.C., was tall and thin where Piers Brendon was the opposite. He shook hands with Arthur and began to explain what would be the course of events.

'Mr Justice Michaelson isn't very fast,' he said, 'but, even so, I wouldn't expect the trial to last above three days. Four at the outside. I think Mr Brendon has told you that, when the time comes, we'll be having a word with you about the advisability or otherwise of your going into the box and giving evidence. It very much depends on how many dents we can make in the prosecution evidence during cross-examination. Some cases gain strength as they proceed, others grow weaker. It's usually unwise to forecast which it'll be. I'm telling you that as I'm sure you're dying to ask me how I rate your chances. The answer is that you must be patient for a bit longer and leave Mr Brendon and myself to do our best for you.'

Arthur nodded and swallowed hard to ease the dry lump he felt in his throat.

It was not long after their departure that he was fetched from his cell and led to the bottom of a narrow flight of steep stairs which kinked out of sight to the left.

'When you get to the top, you'll find yourself in the dock of number one court,' a prison officer said with the relish of a good guide. 'Number one court of the Old Bailey where some of the most famous murderers in history have been tried, not to mention the spies. You ought to feel honoured,' he added jocularly.

'I'm afraid I don't,' Arthur said with an attempt at a smile.

Another officer suddenly appeared where the stairs made their right-angle turn and gestured to his colleague, who gave Arthur a prod in the back.

Halfway up he was halted and told by the other officer to try and sound less like a stampede of buffalo.

From where he now stood, he could see the back of the dock. He also heard the unmistakable sounds of the judge's arrival on the bench.

It wasn't long, however, before he received a further prod and arrived in the dock where he was aware of a sea of faces and barristers' wigs and, immediately ahead of him, a small figure in a scarlet robe with ermine-trimmed sleeves.

Mr Justice Michaelson gave Arthur a melancholy stare from deep-set eyes. His face was heavily lined so as to give him an almost corrugated look. He could have been about a hundred years old, but was, in fact, a mere sixty-three.

'Let the prisoner be arraigned,' he said in a voice as bloodless as his appearance.

Arthur pleaded not guilty and then the clerk of the court started to empanel the jury. Before they could be sworn, however, Mr Justice Michaelson intervened.

There were two women on the prospective jury and it was to them that he addressed himself. One was in her fifties and had rosy cheeks and a comfortable figure. The other must have been at least twenty years younger and was faintly dark-skinned. She wore a permanent half-smile as though enjoying a long private joke and had a generally sinuous appearance.

'I feel I ought to warn you two ladies,' the judge said, 'that this case contains some most unsavoury details which you are likely to find thoroughly distasteful. I have no authority to ask you to stand down; on the other hand if you wished to be excused in the light of what I have just said, I would certainly accede to your request.'

He looked towards the older woman who said robustly, 'I regard myself as shock-proof and am quite prepared to serve.'

His melancholy glance moved to the other woman who returned him a gentle smile. 'Thank you, but I stay, too,' she said.

'Having whetted their appetites what else did he expect?' Brendon whispered to his leader.

'And now they're going to feel let down, unless I've read the wrong brief,' Radley retorted in another whisper.

The jury having been sworn, Arthur was allowed to sit down. A moment later prosecuting counsel rose to make his opening address.

Donald Heague was one of the senior Treasury counsel at the Old Bailey and, as such, was involved in a large number of the more serious cases to reach the court. He was a small, wiry man who overflowed with nervous energy. He hated cases which dragged and was given to making exasperated noises when he felt that opposing counsel lacked his own sense of urgency.

'Members of the jury,' he said, after making the conventional introductions of all the counsel involved, 'this, as his lordship told you a short while ago, is a sordid case. Sordid in detail and squalid as to motive. In brief, the allegation made against the accused is that he murdered a Chinese male prostitute named Tony Ching, he and Ching having been concerned together in blackmailing one of Ching's clients. The client in question was, I am sorry to say, a judge who subsequently committed suicide.

'The evidence is almost entirely circumstantial, but you may not find it difficult to draw the necessary inferences that point to the accused as having committed the crime. Let me say at once that there is no evidence to suggest that the accused himself was one of Ching's clients. They had flats in the same building and the connexion between them was not sexual, but commercial. The commercial exploitation of others . . .'

'Others?' Radley interjected in a tone of outrage. 'What evidence is there of others in the plural?'

'I should have said of a third person,' Heague said testily, patently cross with himself about his slip. 'That third person being, members of the jury, Judge Gerald Wenning who killed himself a few days after Ching's death.'

Arthur listened with fascination and horror as prosecuting counsel constructed the edifice of evidence which constituted the case for the crown. He mentally writhed as Heague invited the jury to draw one false inference after another and yet realised he was powerless to do anything about it. From time to time he glanced at the judge, seeking a sign of comfort but finding none. Mr Justice Michaelson was writing copiously in his notebook, his expression remaining one of melancholy resignation.

As for the jury, they seemed to hang on every word prosecuting counsel uttered. Arthur could only hope that they paid as much attention to his counsel when the moment arrived. There was one juror, a bald-headed man with a half-witted eager expression, who cast Arthur glances of disbelief and disdain as detail followed detail. Arthur decided to put on his own expression of disbelief for the benefit of anyone who looked his way. He wished he could hold aloft a banner which read, 'It sounds awful, doesn't it, but it's not me he's talking about.'

He was relieved when Heague eventually sat down. Surely nothing that happened from now on could be as bad as listening to that concentrated mixture of truth and falsehood. He glanced down at the table in the well of the court that stretched from the dock to the judge's dais. On one side sat Rosa with Francis Radley and Piers Brendon in the front row of counsel's seats immediately behind her. On the opposite side, at the far end, sat Chief Inspector Pennerly and another officer.

The first two witnesses were formal and non-controversial and didn't appear in person. Instead their statements were read out to the court. The next witness was Greg.

Arthur had not seen him since shortly before his, Arthur's, arrest which was now over six months ago. He looked no different, however, save that he had obviously dressed up for the occasion. His short, fair, curly hair had a golden tint in the light which shone immediately over his head. He looked across at Arthur and gave him a tentative smile.

'Kindly take your hand out of your pocket,' Mr Justice Michaelson said in a quiet, unemphatic tone.

'Sorry, I didn't catch,' Greg said, looking around anxiously to identify the voice that had spoken.

'Please remove your hand from your pocket.'

'Oh, yes, of course. Sorry, I didn't notice it was there.'

The judge turned back to his papers with a martyred expression.

It became quickly apparent that Greg would sooner have been anywhere other than the Old Bailey. His nervousness manifested itself in stammered answers and the occasional foolish giggle.

Nobody listened to his evidence with greater attention than Douglas Orden sitting at the back of the court.

When Francis Radley rose to cross-examine, Greg faced him like a rabbit confronted by a ferret.

'Relax, Mr French,' Radley said, 'I'm not going to eat you up!' Avoiding the judge's disapproving look, he went on quickly, 'May I take it that you always regarded Mr Kedby as a good neighbour?'

'Yes,' Greg said with a note of suspicion.

'He was the person whose help you immediately sought on discovering that your friend had been murdered?'

'Yes.'

'You'd scarcely have gone to him unless you trusted him, would you?'

'No.'

'He'd always been kind and helpful to you and Ching?'

'Yes.'

'Can you think of any reason why he should have murdered Tony Ching?'

'No.'

'Had Ching ever said anything to you which suggested he was afraid of Kedby?'

'No.'

'Or mentioned any blackmailing enterprise in which they were engaged together?'

'No,' Greg said quietly, always shaking his head to lend emphasis to his negative replies.

'Do you think you'd have known if they had been so engaged?'

Greg swallowed. 'I don't know.'

'Surely you must have some idea,' Radley remarked with a touch of asperity. 'Did you ever have the impression that he was keeping secrets from you?'

'No.'

'Would he discuss his clients with you?'

'No.'

'Never?'

'Not unless I asked him about them. But generally I didn't want to know.'

'In all the time you knew Kedby, was there ever any suggestion of ill-feeling between him and Ching?'

'No.'

Radley sat down. 'Not exactly a mine of information,' he muttered to Brendon.

Greg vacated the witness box with obvious relief. His forehead glistened with perspiration, but he managed to give Arthur a faint weary smile as he passed the dock.

The next witness was Mrs Barker, the Wennings' next door neighbour. She gave her evidence in a robust and forthright manner, her presence radiating a sense of public duty. When asked if she saw the man she was referring to in her evidence, she pointed an unhesitating finger at Arthur.

'Are you always as certain about everything?' Radley enquired caustically when he rose to cross-examine.

'When I'm certain about something, I say so.'

'That's hardly an answer to my question.'

Mrs Barker gave him a scornful look. 'I have absolutely no doubt that this is the man I saw peering through Judge

Wenning's fence. I had ample opportunity to observe his features and I'm sure I'm not mistaken.'

'Have you never had just the tiniest niggling doubt about it?'

'Never.'

'I see,' Radley said in a thoughtful voice. Then giving the witness a faintly mischievous look, he said, 'What's the colour of the hat you're wearing?'

Mrs Barker's jaw dropped as she stared at him in surprise. 'What's my hat got to do with anything?' she asked indignantly, at the same time putting a hand up to her head.

'You're not sure, are you?'

'Of course I'm sure.'

'But first you hesitated and then you quickly put a hand up either to help you recall its shape or possibly even to check that you were wearing one at all. Isn't that so?'

Leaving the witness glaring furiously at him, Radley sat down, not displeased with his diversionary tactic.

The next two witnesses were the two boys who had seen Arthur emerging from the railway station on his second visit to Gerrards Cross. The first was Adrian Short and he was followed by his friend Gavin Otley.

In the case of witnesses of tender years, judges are required to satisfy themselves that the witness understands the nature and meaning of the oath before allowing him to be sworn. Some judges are more readily persuaded than others, but to Mr Justice Michaelson it was always a serious and onerous duty.

'How old are you?' he asked, fixing Adrian with his melancholy gaze.

'Ten, sir.'

'And do you go to school?'

'Yes, sir,' Adrian said in a tone which suggested he regarded the question as daft.

'Do you read the Bible?'

'No.'

'Have you never read it?' The judge's tone was shocked.

'They read out bits in church,' Adrian said defensively.

'Do you go to church regularly?'

'Sometimes, if Mum and Dad get up in time.'

Mr Justice Michaelson's air of melancholy seemed to grow. 'Do you know what it means to take an oath on the Bible?'

'You swear to tell the truth.'

The judge nodded encouragingly. 'And what happens if you don't tell the truth?'

'You get done for perjury.'

'Good gracious, who told you that?'

'My dad.'

'Can you think of any other reason for telling the truth?'

'No.' The boy glanced about him as if looking for rescue.

'Do you know the difference between right and wrong?' the judge went on relentlessly.

'I think so.'

'You know that it's wrong to tell lies?'

'You shouldn't tell big ones, but everyone tells small ones.'

Mr Justice Michaelson pursed his lips in dismay.

'Serves him right!' Piers Brendon whispered to his leader. 'He shouldn't try and emulate the Spanish Inquisition.'

'Do you promise to tell the truth in this case?' the judge asked despairingly.

'Yes.'

'With not even any small lies?'

'Yes.'

'I am satisfied that he sufficiently understands the meaning of an oath and can be properly sworn,' Mr Justice Michaelson said with a sigh.

When a child witness is good, he is usually very, very

good, being clear-minded and positive. The other sort are so overcome by the occasion that they become speechless and tearful.

It was soon apparent that Adrian belonged to the first category and Radley realised what a difficult ask he faced in cross-examining him. He must be gentle and subtle, for any bullying and browbeating would merely rebound on the defence.

'I expect that since this all happened you and Gavin have talked about it quite a lot, haven't you?' he asked in a friendly tone.

'Quite a lot, yes.'

'And have discussed it with your friends at school?'

'Yes,' Adrian admitted nervously.

'I'm not criticising you, because it was the natural thing to do, but you must have talked about it dozens of times over the past six months, haven't you?'

'I haven't counted,' Adrian said defensively.

'Lots of times then?'

'Yes.'

'Adding little bits here and there to your recollections?'

'I don't understand.'

'I'm sorry, it's my fault for not making my questions as clear as your answers. Very often when one tells the same story over and over again, it changes. Colourful touches are added. Has that happened in this case?'

'I don't know.'

'But it could have?'

'I don't know.'

'Have you and Gavin played detectives since that time?'

'No.'

'Why not?'

'My dad told me to lay off. He said I might get hurt one day.'

'On the day you think you saw this man,' – Radley

gestured towards Arthur – 'did you keep any other people under surveillance?'

'Yes.'

'How many others?'

'I think it was two.'

'Who were they?'

'I don't know.'

'I didn't mean what were their names, but can you describe them?'

'One was a lady.'

'What was she wearing?'

'A coat.'

'What colour was it?'

'Red, I think.'

'But you're not sure?'

'No.'

'And what was she doing?'

'She went in and out of the shops.'

'Which shops?'

'I can't remember.'

'Would you recognise her if you saw her again?'

'I might do.'

'And who was the other person whose movements you kept watch on that day?'

Adrian bit his lip and looked close to tears. 'I don't remember.'

'That's all right,' Radley said sympathetically. 'Don't get upset about it. If you can't remember, you can't remember.'

It seemed a good moment to end his cross-examination and he sat down.

Gavin Otley followed his friend into the witness-box. He was a much shyer boy than Adrian and it was soon apparent which of them was the leader and which the willing disciple.

Mr Justice Michaelson once more embarked upon a

religious inquisition, but brought it to a benign conclusion after the boy had disclosed that his father was himself a minister of religion.

Though his evidence tallied with that of his friend, it was given with less assurance.

When Radley stood up to cross-examine, Gavin readily agreed that he and Adrian had discussed their adventure on many occasions. He also acknowledged that he had hesitated at the identification parade before picking out Arthur.

'What made you hesitate?' Radley asked gently.

'I don't know.'

'Would it have been because you weren't sure?'

'Yes.'

'And are you still not absolutely sure?'

'Not absolutely.'

'Did Adrian describe to you afterwards the man he had picked out?'

'Yes.'

'How many other people did you keep under observation that day, Gavin?'

'I can't remember.'

'One? Two? Three?'

'I think it was three.'

'Can you describe any of them now?'

'No.'

'Why not?'

'It was a long time ago.'

'That's certainly true. Do you remember whether they were men or women?'

'I remember a woman.'

'What was she wearing?'

'A hat.'

'What colour was the hat?'

'I can't remember.'

'Did she have on a coat?'

'I don't remember.'

'Would you recognise her if you saw her again?'

'I don't think so. Oh, and there was a man with a white moustache who looked like a colonel.'

'What was he doing?'

'He went into a betting shop.'

'Where did he go when he came out?'

'He didn't come out.'

Gavin looked round in anxious surprise at the ripple of mirth his answer caused. Only the judge remained impassive.

Radley deemed it a good moment to sit down. He was aware that he had done little to shake the basic substance of their evidence, but he hoped he might have cast some doubt on their infallibility as witnesses of Arthur's identity.

By the time the court rose at the end of the day, the crown had called much of its evidence.

'Police evidence will take up the whole of tomorrow morning,' he remarked to Rosa, as they gathered up their papers. 'And that means, if we don't call Kedby, we could be into speeches by the afternoon and the case could finish the following day.'

'But I thought you were proposing to make a submission at the close of the crown case,' Rosa said.

'I am.' With a faint smile, he added, 'I'm afraid I was discounting its success.'

'I'm not sure you're right to do so,' Brendon chimed in. 'There really are some gaping holes in the prosecution evidence.'

'I know, but it takes a strong judge to uphold a submission of no case in a trial such as this and I doubt whether Hector Michaelson is such a judge. It's always easier to throw the bone to the jury and let them gnaw at it.'

'I must say I've never come across a judge who gives so little indication of his view,' Brendon said. 'He doesn't give a clue as to what's going on behind that crinkled parchment façade.'

'Except for an obvious deploring of our moral decay,' Rosa said crisply. She closed her briefcase. 'I'd better go and have a word with Kedby before he's taken back to Brixton.'

'I don't think either of us need accompany you,' Radley observed. 'Tell him we'll have a word with him in the morning.'

'How do you think it's going?' Arthur asked eagerly as soon as Rosa appeared.

'The main thing is that there haven't been any nasty surprises sprung on us and Mr Radley has managed to dent the credibility of some of the witnesses.'

Arthur nodded. 'You couldn't have picked a better pair than him and Mr Brendon.'

'I'm glad you're satisfied,' Rosa remarked drily. 'Incidentally, Mr Radley thinks the trial should end the day after tomorrow.'

'Have they said any more about my giving evidence?'

'They still haven't decided.'

'Why don't they want me to?'

'They've never said that.'

'No, but I can tell they'd sooner avoid it if possible.'

'It's only because you are rather vulnerable to cross-examination in view of the strength of the identity witnesses.'

Arthur passed his tongue slowly over his lips. 'I guessed that was it.' He gave Rosa a beseeching look. 'You believe me, don't you, Miss Epton?'

'My belief is neither here nor there,' she said with a sigh. 'We've been through all this before.'

'But you do, don't you? Please tell me you do!'

'I refuse to answer such a question.'

'Which means that you don't believe me.'

'Now, don't put on a self-pitying act. The case has so

far gone as well as we could hope and that should be good news to you.' Observing Arthur's still self-indulgent expression, she added, 'You wouldn't expect a surgeon to rave over your vital organs, so you mustn't expect me to be any less clinical in handling your defence.'

But Arthur did and it continued to rankle with him that he had failed to secure Rosa's belief in his innocence. From the first moment he had met her, he had wanted her to believe in him and saw the fact that he had told her a string of lies as quite irrelevant.

On arrival back at the prison, he found himself once more beside Ralphie Earle as they waited in the reception area. Earle was looking as jumpy as a marionette in a stiff breeze.

'My bloody trial almost didn't start,' he muttered darkly to Arthur. ''Ung around in the cells till 'alf past three, I did. Bloody liberty if you ask me!'

Arthur could think of no more enlightened comment than, 'Oh!'

'What about you, mate?'

'All right.'

'What sort of judge?'

'Mr Justice Michaelson.'

'Never 'eard of 'im. Mine's a real ripe bastard. Don't know 'is name, but 'e's a bloody stinker. Got my bloody lawyer on the run in the first ten minutes, 'e did. Useless bloody twerp!'

'Oh, well, better luck tomorrow,' Arthur said, deciding he had had enough of his foxy companion for one day.

Earle shot him a suspicious glance, followed by one of his sly winks. 'Yeah,' he said, 'it could be different termorrer.'

CHAPTER 20

Douglas Orden had promised his wife that he would visit her mother while in London for the trial, but had resisted the suggestion that he should put up at her flat. He said he preferred to be independent and proposed to stay at the small hotel off Gloucester Road which he and Christine had used on a number of occasions when obliged to spend a night in town.

Accordingly he had phoned Diana and arranged to take her out to dinner on his first evening.

When he arrived at her flat around seven o'clock, she greeted him with the news that Christine had been trying to reach him and wanted him to call her before they went out to the restaurant.

'She said she tried to get you at the hotel, but you weren't in,' his mother-in-law remarked as she led the way into her sitting room.

'I only dashed in for a wash and then came straight round here.' He sighed. 'I suppose I'd better call her.'

'You can use the phone in my bedroom,' Diana said. 'It'll be more private.'

He made a deprecating face, but nevertheless walked towards the door. If Christine began talking about her mother, it would be embarrassing to have her sitting at his elbow.

'I gather you've been trying to get in touch with me,' he said militantly as soon as he heard his wife's voice on the line.

'Is Mummy in the room with you?' she asked immediately in a lowered voice.

'No, I'm in the bedroom.'

'How did the trial go?'

'All right.'

'Was Daddy's name dragged through the mire?'

'No.'

'That's a relief. I suppose Kedby hasn't given evidence yet?'

'No. So far it's been defending counsel trying to punch holes in the prosecution case.'

'Is our counsel there?'

'Yes. He's taking notes as if his career depended on it.'

'Did you speak to him?'

'Briefly.' There was a pause and he said, 'By the way, how's business been?'

'Only two people in all day and they just had a thorough look around before walking out again.'

'Well, if that's all, I'd better get back to your mother.'

'There is one other matter. Percy Sugarman phoned this evening.'

'From Spain?'

'Yes.'

'What's he want?'

'He said he wanted to talk to you and will you call him back later tonight. He said you had his number.' Douglas grunted. 'Do you have any idea what he wants?' Christine asked suspiciously.

'How can I have?'

'I thought he might have been calling by arrangement.' When her husband made no comment, she went on, 'Where are you taking Mummy to dinner?'

'That Greek place round the corner.'

'Oh! I thought you might be taking her somewhere slap-up.'

'*She* seems quite happy with my choice,' he said tartly. When, shortly afterwards, he returned to the sitting room, he said in a tone with a slight edge to it, 'Your daughter appears to think I'm taking you slumming.'

'What nonsense! I like little Mr Kestides and I'm also fond of Greek food. Moreover, it's small and quiet. In fact, just the place to take a mother-in-law.'

Douglas grinned. He had never disliked Diana and there were actual moments when he positively liked her.

It was towards the end of the meal when she remarked suddenly, 'I hope it was the man on trial who killed that Chinaman.' Douglas gave her a startled look and she added, 'I wouldn't like to think that the police may have got the wrong person.'

'There's no reason for thinking that at all,' he said with a frown.

'I certainly hope not.'

'What's on your mind?' he asked when she fell silent.

'You don't think it might have been Gerald?' Observing his expression, she went on, 'It's not all that far-fetched and murder would merely have been the penultimate step in his final disintegration. After that, only suicide was left. I know I told the police he was at home on the evening of the murder, but at the time I felt I had to say so. I don't, in fact, know whether he was or he wasn't. He could have gone out for a couple of hours, I simply don't remember.' She gazed across at the dessert trolley. 'Now let's talk about something else. I hadn't really intended bringing it up, except that the trial is the reason for your visit to London.' Her gaze came back to his face. 'I must be strong-minded. I'll just have coffee.'

Douglas was still brooding on what she had said when he arrived back at the hotel. He went straight up to his room and undressed before putting through a call to Spain.

Percy Sugarman greeted him with customary ebullience. 'You don't know what you're missing, Doug. I'm sitting out on the patio with a brandy and a big cigar. You and Chris would love it out 'ere.'

'What was it you wanted to talk about?' Douglas asked tetchily.

'You O.K., Doug? You sound kind of edgy.'

'I'm fine.'

'I wanted to know 'ow the trial's going?'

'It only began today. So far there've not been any surprises.'

'Glad to 'ear that, Doug. What's the defence up to?'

'Nothing startling.'

'Good, good! Let's hope it stays like that, eh, Doug? By the way, I was talking to Ron earlier this evening. Remember me telling you about Ralphie Earle? His trial's also started.'

'Oh!'

'Well, I mustn't keep you, Doug, from whatever it is you're about to do,' he said, with a leer in his voice.

'As a matter of fact I'm about to go to bed.'

'That sounds like a waste of a good evening. Anyway, thought I'd call you and say hello.'

Except it's me who is doing the calling and paying, Douglas reflected sourly.

In many ways he would like to loosen his ties with the Sugarmans, though this was something that was easier said than done. Moreover, he might still have need of their help.

CHAPTER 21

When Arthur arrived at court the next day he was put into a different cell.

'This isn't the one I was in yesterday,' he said to the escorting officer, rather as if he were a guest being shown to the wrong hotel bedroom.

'Your trial's been shifted from number one court,' the officer said, without explanation.

'Why?'

'Because it has, that's why!'

About half an hour later, Rosa and his two counsel appeared.

'As you've probably realised, we'll be in a different court today,' Radley said.

'Why's that?' Arthur asked.

'I've no idea, but it's not uncommon.' He gave Arthur a thin smile. 'It won't affect the quality of justice. We'll see how things go this morning before deciding about your evidence. It's very likely I'll decide to make a submission of no case to answer at the close of the prosecution. If it's upheld, then that'll be an end of the trial, but I don't want to raise your hopes because I'm doubtful whether it'll succeed. In which event we shall have to decide whether or not you should give evidence. My present inclination is still to advise you against, but there's no need yet to make a final decision.'

The first witness of the day was the clerk from the Trafalgar Square Post Office. He was a pale-faced young man with dark rings round his eyes and an Adam's apple that was working overtime before he even finished taking the oath.

'I know I picked the defendant out at the identification parade, but it was only with difficulty and it's been worrying me ever since. I really shouldn't have done so, as I wasn't a bit sure.' With an apologetic air, he went on, 'I see dozens of faces in the course of a day and I don't remember a fraction of them afterwards. I didn't want to attend the parade, but the police insisted. I'm sorry if I've let anyone down, but the whole thing's become a nightmare. I've even had to go and see a doctor about my nerves.'

As Arthur listened, he felt it was his first piece of good fortune since the trial had begun. He dare not, however, so much as glance in the direction of the witness for fear he should suddenly exclaim that he now recognised him perfectly after all.

When prosecuting counsel eventually sat down, Radley informed the court that he had no wish to cross-examine.

Mr Justice Michaelson, who had shown no reaction while the witness was squirming unhappily under crown counsel's questioning, now fixed him with a sad stare.

'I trust,' he said, 'that your experience here today will have taught you the necessity of resisting blandishments, from whatever quarter they come, to give evidence of matters about which you're uncertain.'

The witness' Adam's apple made a final agitated bob.

'Yes, sir, it has,' he stammered, before gratefully relinquishing the limelight.

'That seemed a bit uncalled for,' Brendon muttered to his leader.

'*His* trouble is that *he* can never resist the opportunity to moralise.'

Meanwhile, Detective Chief Inspector Pennerly was left glowering at the table where he was sitting. How did the silly old fool think anyone was ever got to give evidence without blandishments of one kind or another!

The handwriting expert, who was the next witness, was a stooped figure with a mass of white hair which seemed to sprout outwards in every direction.

'I don't imagine that you would lay any claim to infallibility?' Radley said pleasantly, when he rose to cross-examine.

'Oh, dear me, no!' the witness replied with a chuckle. 'In case you didn't know, sir, there are two sorts of expert witnesses and that's the other sort.' He glanced around with a toothy smile which faded when it met Mr Justice Michaelson's reproving look.

'Am I right in thinking that ballpoint pens reveal fewer of the writer's characteristics than any other type of pen?'

'Yes, but they still show some. For example, as to pressure.'

'But you found only one such point of similarity in your examination of the two envelopes and the defendant's handwriting specimen, did you not?'

'That's quite correct, sir.'

'So we can virtually exclude pressure as an identifying characteristic in this case?'

'Except for the instance I've mentioned.'

'You're saying that the letter "J" in the word Judge in each of the three exhibits was, in your view, formed with the same degree of pressure?'

'Precisely.'

'It's the first letter of the first word in each case, is it not?'

'It is indeed.'

'Isn't it natural to press harder at the beginning in order to make sure the pen will write?'

'Yes, but here it was the identical degree of pressure that persuaded me that the same hand had written all three items.'

'Can you really measure it that accurately?'

'I'm pleased to think so.'

'But you could be mistaken?'

'As I said to you earlier, I've never claimed infallibility,' the witness said with another toothy grin.

'So the effect of your evidence hinges on the single letter "J"?'

'That's the one positive feature, but the absence of any negative features is also significant. There's nothing to suggest that the same person could not have written all three items.'

Radley resumed his seat. 'I'm sure he's a clever man,' he said in an aside to Brendon, 'but that doesn't mean he's a clever witness.'

Shortly before the lunch adjournment, Pennerly went into the witness-box, but it was late afternoon before Radley began his cross-examination.

'How many days elapsed between your first interview with the defendant and his being charged?'

'Eleven.'

'Did you always suspect him?'

'No, I had an open mind at the outset of the investigation.'

'How many of Ching's clients have you interviewed?'

'About a dozen.'

'But one presumes he had many more than that?'

'Yes, but we could only interview those we could trace and we could only trace those whose telephone numbers we found in his book.'

'Did all of those you traced have an alibi for the night of the murder?'

Pennerly pursed his lips. 'I don't think I can answer that with a yes or a no.'

'Answer it as best you can.'

'Some had alibis which we could substantiate, others didn't. And a few had no idea what they were doing that evening, save that they were sure they didn't visit the deceased.'

'At any rate, they all denied having any part in his death?'

'Yes.'

'But that still leaves many others you've not been able to trace?'

'Yes.'

'And who could have murdered him?'

'It was a possibility that was always in my mind.'

'And still is?'

'I can't exclude it altogether, but I no longer regard it as a reasonable possibility.'

'Did it ever occur to you that Judge Wenning might have killed Ching?'

Pennerly gave the judge a hasty glance before replying. 'Yes, but his wife told me he was at home all that evening.'

'How was she able to remember?'

Pennerly shifted uncomfortably and cast Mr Justice Michaelson another glance, but the judge didn't look up from his notebook.

'I accepted her word,' he said stonily.

'Just like that?'

'I don't follow you, sir.'

'You didn't try and find any outside evidence to support what she had told you?'

'I did, but there wasn't any.'

'I see,' Radley said thoughtfully. Giving his gown a hitch, he fixed the witness with a long, hard stare. 'I suggest to you, Mr Pennerly, that, faced with a multitude of suspects, you, so to speak, reached out and grabbed the nearest.'

Rosa had been listening to the cross-examination while at the same time leafing through Judge Wenning's pocket diary. It had been produced as an exhibit by the crown to prove his link with Tony Ching, whose bare telephone number appeared on a back page. She had examined the diary at the magistrates' court with other original exhibits, but was now giving it a further scrutiny. Her attention was caught by a list of sums and jotted abbreviations which Pennerly had told her he believed to relate to gambling wins and losses. Among them was one which didn't seem to conform with the rest. It read '2½gdoret' and she was staring at it with a puzzled frown when she became aware that Pennerly had not replied to counsel's last question.

She glanced towards the witness-box in time to see him staring up at the public gallery with an expression of frozen horror.

'Lie down everybody,' he yelled suddenly.

There was a crash as if a lump of metal had landed in court, followed almost immediately by a violent explosion.

Without any recollection of getting there, Rosa found herself beneath the heavy table. There was a strong smell of cordite and her ears were singing like telephone wires in a wind. Bits and pieces were raining down on the floor and on the table over her head. A little later she observed a pair of legs walking past her line of vision and she cautiously crawled out from her shelter. As she did so, a number of heads popped up from cover. She glanced towards the judge who was slumped sideways in his chair with an expression of surprise on his face.

A pall of acrid smoke hung in the still air of the court-room and every surface seemed to be littered with splinters of wood and shredded upholstery.

A number of people were moaning and one or two were crying out in pain.

'Somebody in the public gallery threw a grenade,' a reporter said to her, but had to shout it before she heard.

She moved unsteadily to where she could peer into the dock. It resembled the scene of a massacre. Arthur Kedby and the two prison officers lay corpselike on the floor.

'Make way, I'm a doctor,' somebody said, pushing her gently aside.

She returned to her seat to find the chair on which she had been sitting looking as if it had been attacked with a hatchet. It was with relief that she found both Francis Radley and Piers Brendon unharmed, though she suddenly noticed that the latter had the beginnings of a black eye.

'It's all right,' he said with a rueful smile. 'My face got in the way of Francis's shoe as we dived for cover.' He glanced towards the bench. 'It looks as if the judge has come round,' he added. 'I definitely saw him blink just then.'

'Who could have thrown it?' she asked in a dulled tone.

'God knows, or why!'

The dock now seemed to be full of people and one of them, a uniformed officer normally on duty at the door, leaned over and spoke to her.

'I'm afraid your client's had it, Miss Epton. Looks as if the base pin caught him in the back of the neck. At least he wouldn't have known what happened.'

'What about the officers with him?'

'One's badly hurt, but the other appears to have got away with superficial cuts.'

Rosa shivered uncontrollably. It was her first experience of the aftermath of battle, for that was what it amounted to.

Within a few minutes, a number of officers arrived in court and a superintendent of the City of London police

162

took charge. The toll to date appeared to be one dead, one seriously injured, six less seriously injured (mostly from flying splinters) and eight with minor injuries.

About twenty minutes later, Pennerly returned to court.

'I'm afraid the chap who threw it got away in the confusion,' he said to Rosa and others who greeted his return. 'But at least we've got a good description.'

'But what was it all in aid of?' Brendon asked.

'My guess is that it was intended to create a diversion to enable a prisoner to escape. Not the unfortunate Kedby, but a man named Earle whose trial began in this court yesterday, but which was moved to another court for security reasons. Earle belongs to a gang who'd be capable of this sort of thing. Whoever was responsible obviously didn't realise his case had been transferred from this court.'

'It's lucky for him or he'd have been dead by now instead of Kedby,' Brendon remarked.

'I gather that the chap who threw the grenade only entered the public gallery a few seconds beforehand. He just darted to the front and tossed it down. But the man sitting next to where he stood realised that something was up and gave him a push which must have deflected his aim.' He glanced at the faces around him. 'But for that, there'd have been worse casualties, including some of you. As it was, it fell into the confined space of the dock and exploded there.' He gave Rosa a wry look. 'I feel like saying that poetic justice has been done, Miss Epton, but I don't expect you'd agree.'

She shook her head. 'Not even Old Testament justice,' she said.

Detective Sergeant Allen, who had been outside court waiting to give his evidence, now appeared at Pennerly's side.

'They think the chap got away on a motor-cycle,' he said. 'Somebody was seen to sprint from the court and get on one which was parked round the corner. He accelerated away as if all the demons in hell were on his tail.'

'Did anyone get the registration number?' Pennerly asked.

'We've got part of it.'

Pennerly gave a satisfied nod and turned to the clerk of the court who had just joined them.

'The judge is in his room,' the clerk said. 'He seems to have lost his hearing, but is otherwise unharmed. Anyway, he won't be coming back on the bench so you can all go home as far as the court is concerned.' He turned towards the jury box to impart his message to their depleted ranks.

By the time Rosa was ready to leave, the whole of London had been made aware of the outrage via radio and television and she had to run the gauntlet of reporters and photographers. To her enormous joy, she found that Robin Snaith had arrived in his car to fetch her.

'You'd better stay at home for a couple of days,' he said as they drove off.

'I can't. Anyway, I'm perfectly all right, or shall be once I've had a bath and washed all the dirt out of my hair. I'm absolutely filthy. I even found a splinter of wood inside my blouse.'

'You could suffer from delayed shock,' he said.

'Not me. I'm tough.'

'I know you are, but . . .'

'There's something I have to follow up immediately, Robin.'

'Can't I do it for you?'

She shook her head. 'I must have another look at Judge Wenning's diary. I was studying it when the grenade was thrown. I wonder what happened to it. I hope to goodness it wasn't destroyed in the blast.'

Later that evening she was relieved to learn that it had been swept up by a cleaner and retrieved from a pile of debris by Sergeant Allen.

CHAPTER 22

As soon as Christine heard the news flash on the portable radio she carried from room to room when she was alone, she dashed to the phone to call her mother.

'Have you heard what's happened at the Old Bailey?' she asked, striving to keep a note of hysteria out of her voice.

'In that trial, you mean?' her mother said in a puzzled tone.

'A bomb went off in the court. I've just heard a news flash.'

'How awful! But there are lots of courts there, it may . . .'

'No, no, it said it was in the court where Kedby was on trial. You haven't had a call from Douglas?'

'No, but I'm sure he'll be calling you as soon as he can,' Diana said reassuringly.

'It said there were many injured,' Christine went on desperately.

'You mustn't imagine that Douglas is amongst them. I expect he's quite all right, but can't get to a phone. He may even be trying to ring you at this moment.' She paused. 'Was anyone killed?'

'Certainly one and possibly more.'

'I suppose it was the I.R.A. again.'

'It didn't say, but why should they set off a bomb in that court? Hold on, Mummy, there's another news flash coming through, I'll turn up the sound.' Diana could hear a distant voice and then her daughter came back on the line. 'It wasn't a bomb after all. Somebody in the public gallery threw a grenade. I pray that Douglas wasn't hurt. I don't know why he ever wanted to attend the trial,' she said vehemently. 'I told him it wasn't necessary for him to be there, but he insisted on going. Well, I'd better get off the line in case he's trying to call me.'

'Let me know as soon as you hear from him. And don't worry, I'm sure he's all right.'

Diana Wenning stood staring out of the window for some time after she had put down the receiver. It seemed as if her husband's behaviour had really stirred up the furies.

From his seat at the back of the court, Douglas had heard Pennerly's shout and had then actually seen the grenade strike the top of the dock and bounce in, though he had no idea what it was. But when he saw people ducking for cover, he followed suit. After the explosion he was one of the first to get to his feet again. He noticed a splinter of metal embedded in the wall immediately behind where he'd been sitting.

Dazed and shocked, he staggered out of court without anyone trying to stop him. His only aim was to get away from the court. He walked down the street and entered a café where he bought a cup of extra strong tea. Before he had time to lift it to his lips, the air outside was filled with the urgent sound of sirens as police cars, ambulances and fire appliances hurtled towards the building.

All he sought at the moment was anonymity and time to recover his thoughts. He was thankful that there was nothing in his physical appearance to give away his recent presence at the scene.

He had no reason to doubt that the grenade had been deliberately thrown and intentionally aimed. The obvious inference was that somebody had been determined to silence Arthur Kedby. But why? He regarded it as significant that it had happened shortly before Kedby was due to give evidence (it had not entered his mind that Kedby might not do so) and he therefore inferred it must be related to that event. It was this inference that occupied his thoughts as he sat sipping tea the colour of rich mahogany.

When, some fifteen minutes later, he left the café, he glanced back towards the Old Bailey which, by now, gave the impression of being under siege.

After walking some distance, he found a taxi and gave the driver the address of his Kensington hotel.

'Oh, Mr Orden,' the receptionist gushed as he approached the desk. 'What a relief to see you all right! Your wife's been constantly on the phone. She sounded so worried about you. Shall I get her number for you straight away?'

'I'll call her from my room in a moment,' he said.

'It must have been a terrible experience. We heard about it on the news, of course, but we had no idea you were there until your wife rang. There was also a call for you from Spain, from a Mr Sugarman. He wished you to phone him back if you came in . . . I mean, as soon as you came in. Well, I mustn't detain you, Mr Orden. Here's your key.'

When he reached his room, the first thing he did was to plunge his face into a bowl of cold water. It was while he was drying it that the phone rang and he walked over to the bedside table to answer it.

'Oh, darling, are you all right?' Christine exclaimed almost before the receiver reached his ear. 'I've been worried out of my mind about you.'

'Well, you can stop worrying now,' he said firmly,

'because I'm all right. I only arrived back a few minutes ago and was about to call you.'

'Tell me exactly what happened,' she said in an urgent voice.

'I'd sooner not talk about it now. I've got rather a headache and I'm going to lie down for a while.'

'But you said you were all right.'

'I am, apart from the headache,' he said with a trace of impatience.

'Will you be coming home this evening?'

'I think I'd better stop here for the night.'

'Shall I drive up and fetch you?' she enquired anxiously.

'No, I'd just like to rest for a bit. I'll call you later this evening or tomorrow morning.'

'But, darling, I hate to think of you being there on your own. Are you sure you wouldn't like me to drive up?'

'No. I promise you I'll be all right, so don't worry. It's just that I don't want to have to talk about it to anyone.'

'Shall I get Mummy to ask her doctor to come round and see you?'

'Please, no! I don't need a doctor.'

'You could be suffering from delayed shock without realising it,' she said, being now certain in her own mind that this explained his somewhat curious reaction to her phone call.

'I'm not. Now let me get some rest, love, as my head's splitting.'

'I really do think I ought to drive up,' she said unhappily.

'Be a good girl and stop arguing. I know what's best for me.'

As soon as Christine had rung off, he put through a call to Percy Sugarman. Lorraine, his wife, answered, but said Percy was only sitting out on the patio and that she would fetch him.

' 'Ello, Doug, you O.K.? We 'eard the news on the

radio. We always tune in to the B.B.C. I gather you weren't 'urt, but what a to-do!'

'I'm still feeling a bit dazed.'

'I bet. Why don't you fly out 'ere for a bit of a break? You could do with one after that. What was it all about?'

'I'm still wondering.'

'Sounds like somebody didn't want Kedby to give evidence.'

'That's my inference, too.'

'Hmm!' After a pause, Percy went on in a thoughtful tone, 'Mind you, I don't like mysteries, unless I start 'em, but one 'as to admit that this 'as tidied up the case very nicely.'

The next morning when Douglas bought a newspaper and read that a police spokesman was suggesting the grenade had probably been intended to disrupt a quite different trial, but that the perpetrator had made a serious miscalculation, he, too, felt that it had tidied up the case rather nicely.

CHAPTER 23

As soon as Robin Snaith had dropped her at her flat on Campden Hill, Rosa had a long, luxurious hot bath, after which she felt considerably restored. Although she had been in the flat for only three months and it was tiny, it represented her first real home and she cherished it accordingly. Before that she had always shared with others who came and departed like refugees in a transit camp and all the while she had longed for a place of her own.

Wrapped in an absurdly large dressing-gown which had once belonged to her brother, she poured herself a glass of cold Chambéry and sat down to think to the background accompaniment of the waltz theme from *Der Rosenkavalier*.

Her copy of the exhibits hadn't included a photostat of the page of Judge Wenning's diary she had been studying when the grenade went off, but she had memorised the entry that had been puzzling her. She now wrote it down and stared at it with furrowed concentration – '2½gdoret'.

It was quite different from the other entries on the page, which appeared to relate to bets. The page in question was a cash account for the month of October and the mysterious entry had been almost the last. She seemed to remember that there were only two others after it. It was therefore a reasonable inference that it referred to something which had taken place only shortly before Judge Wenning's death.

She recalled that in the second before the grenade exploded, she had been wondering whether '2½g' could stand for '2½ grand', namely £2,500. If it did, it was far in excess of any other amount that appeared on the page, the next highest being £250.

But if that was a correct deduction what did 'doret' with a small 'd' mean? Could it be the name of some spectacular horse that had never lost a race and which justified a substantial bet? It seemed unlikely.

It was at this moment that a narrow, handsome face with eager, observant eyes popped up in her mind. She had met Bob Tyre at a party a few weeks earlier and they had amused each other sufficiently to exchange telephone numbers. But what was now suddenly important to her was his job as a racing correspondent. She found his number and dialled it.

'That you, Eddie, you rotten bugger?' he said as he lifted the receiver.

'I'm afraid not. It's Rosa Epton. We met . . .'

'At a terrible party where we were the only interesting couple.'

'I wasn't sure if you'd remember me.'

'Beautiful Rosa with the lovely eyes and the hair that fell enchantingly forward to hide your blushes. I was about to call you and invite you out to dinner.'

Rosa thought this was probably one of his more frequent lines of dialogue and decided to ignore it.

'I need your professional help, Bob,' she said. 'Can you tell me whether a horse named Doret ran in any races last October?'

'If you hold on, I can answer that quite quickly.' A few moments later he was back on the line. 'How do you spell it?'

'D-O-R-E-T.'

'No such animal according to my records. Horses have some pretty strange names, but that one doesn't strike a chord.'

'That's that then! Thanks for the information.'

'What about having dinner with me?'

'I'd like to, but can we leave it for a week or two?'

'Sure, that suits me, too. I'm going to be out of London a good deal over the next few days. Incidentally, what about that explosion at the Old Bailey this afternoon? I trust you weren't anywhere near.'

'As a matter of fact, I was.'

'Not in the actual court where it happened?'

'Yes.'

'You were?' he said incredulously. 'How about an exclusive interview, Rosa?'

'I thought you only interviewed horses.'

'No, I mean it.'

'Sorry, but no.'

'Oh, come on.'

'I'll give you full details when we meet for dinner.'

'But it'll be as stale as last week's bread by then.'

'I know,' she said, and quickly rang off.

In fact, her evening was several times interrupted by calls from the press, but each received a polite but effective brush-off.

By the time she went to bed, her head had begun to spin from trying to make sense of the cryptic diary entry. If Doret was not a horse, then it seemed unlikely that '$2\frac{1}{2}$g' stood for £2,500.

First thing the next morning she would phone Pennerly and try and enlist his help – or, rather, excite his interest. She wasn't very optimistic about doing so as she realised he would be only too ready to regard the case as now closed.

Pennerly looked dog-tired. It showed most in his eyes and his voice, when he spoke, sounded hoarse.

'I'm afraid I have to go out in half an hour, Miss Epton,' he said uncompromisingly, almost as soon as Rosa entered his office. With a faint note of belligerence, he added, 'And I've been up most of the night.'

'Have you made an arrest yet?'

He shook his head. 'No, but it's only a question of time. We now know who we're looking for. He was contracted by the Goodbody gang to spring Earle, but a right cock-up he made of it. However, that's not what you've come to see me about.'

'I wanted to have a look at exhibit three, Wenning's diary.'

'We photographed the only relevant page. The one with Ching's number on it.'

'I'm interested in another page.'

Pennerly looked at her sharply. 'Am I allowed to know which?'

'Of course. I'd like your help, anyway.'

He got up and went across to a steel cupboard from which he produced a carton labelled, *Exhibits: R.v. Kedby.* Carrying it over to his desk, he reached in for the diary and handed it to Rosa.

'It's this,' she said, pointing at the entry with her finger.

'2½-g-d-o-r-e-t,' he read out loud to himself.

'What does it mean?'

'Presumably it relates to some betting matter,' he said in a faintly bored tone.

'All the other entries on the page appear to, but this one's quite different.'

He gave a shrug. 'Even so, does it matter?'

'I want to find out what it means,' she said stubbornly.

His expression suddenly brightened. 'It means he put a bet of two and a half grand on a horse called Doret.'

'There's no horse of that name.'

'How do you know?' Quickly he went on, 'All right, don't tell me, I suppose you've already checked.'

'Yes. It looks as if the entry was made only shortly before his death.'

'I don't know what you mean by shortly, but it's certainly one of the last on the page for October.'

'And that was the month he committed suicide.'

'O.K., so what?'

'I still want to find out what it means.'

'Why?'

'Because I think it may be important.'

He looked at her with a mixture of curiosity and irritation. 'Important to whom?'

'To truth and therefore to my late client.'

'And so you now want me to help you prove he was innocent all the time?' he enquired in a faintly hectoring tone.

'I happen to believe he was innocent. I haven't much doubt that he wrote those two envelopes and I strongly suspect that they contained blackmailing letters, but I don't believe he murdered Ching.'

'Look, Miss Epton,' he said wearily, 'Ching is dead, Judge Wenning's dead, and now your client's dead, can't we leave it there?'

'No.'

'I shouldn't have said his death was poetic justice and I apologise, but nothing's going to bring him back to life. Maybe he would have been acquitted, I don't know, but the case is now over and finished.'

'If he had been eventually acquitted, would you have left it at that?'

'Certainly, in default of any additional evidence to justify further enquiries.'

'So you're not interested in this unexplained diary entry?'

'Why should I be? I believe your client was a murderer

as well as a blackmailer and it'll take more than a cryptic entry in a diary to persuade me otherwise.'

'So you won't investigate it?'

'There are probably other cryptic entries if you look, but I'm not interested in any of them unless they can be shown to be relevant to the charge we brought against Kedby.'

'In the first place there aren't any others because I've looked and in the second how do you know this one's not relevant if you don't know what it means?'

He let out an exasperated sigh. 'Surely you don't expect me to chase hares just to satisfy your curiosity.'

'It isn't merely to satisfy my curiosity. However, I can see I've not persuaded you it's worth further investigation.'

'I'm sorry, but you haven't.'

'I'll have to see what I can find out myself.'

'Oh, lord, are you that determined?'

'Yes. And if I get anywhere, I shall come and present you with my findings. Perhaps you'll then feel obliged to give the matter your official attention.'

'You really are throwing down the gauntlet, aren't you?' he remarked.

Rosa smiled. 'I suppose you can see it that way, but I assure you it's without any personal animosity. After all, if it hadn't been for you, Mr Pennerly, I'd have been sitting at the table, instead of crouching under it, when the grenade went off. In that event, it's unlikely I'd now be sitting in your office. So thank you.'

Pennerly grinned. 'You're very good at disarming people, Miss Epton. As to your own detective work, I shall be very happy to hear the result if you ever manage to solve the mystery of $2\frac{1}{2}$g whatever it is.'

'Don't worry, you will. One final thing, will you lend me the diary for a few days?' Observing his expression she added quickly, 'You can always say I took it from your desk without permission. I won't dispute that.' Seeing him still hesitate, she went on, 'After all, it's no longer a court exhibit and it's only awaiting disposal when you get round to it.'

'You're quite one of the most persistent solicitors I've ever met.'

'Thank you.'

'I'm not sure I meant it as a compliment.'

'I'm sure you didn't, but I took it as one.'

'O.K., but I must have it back within a week. And don't tamper with it in any way!'

'You shall and I won't.'

'Incidentally, where are you going to start your enquiries?'

'At the obvious place.'

'Which is?'

'Mrs Wenning.'

Rosa had made a note of Diana Wenning's new address when she read through the bundle of statements of persons the crown was not proposing to call as witnesses and which had been made available to the defence on a counsel-to-counsel basis.

'Mrs Wenning?' she said to the woman who peered at her round the edge of the door which was still on its chain.

'If you're from a newspaper, I have nothing to say.'

'I'm not. I'm a solicitor. I was acting for the man who was killed in court yesterday.'

'What do you want?'

'I'd like to have a quiet talk to you, Mrs Wenning.'

The chain was removed and the door held open for Rosa to enter. Diana Wenning then led the way into her sitting room.

'My name's Rosa Epton and I'm a partner in the firm of Snaith and Epton,' Rosa said when they were seated.

'Were you in court when the thing exploded?' Diana asked, staring at her with curiosity.

'Yes, but I managed to get under a table in time.'

'My son-in-law was also there.'

'Oh! I don't think I've met him. I hope he wasn't injured.'

'No, he also escaped unhurt. I gather from the papers it was all a mistake. It was meant to happen in another court.'

'The police are sure of it.' Rosa opened her shoulder bag and brought out the diary. 'I expect you recognise this, Mrs Wenning, it's your late husband's diary. I'm wondering if you can help clear up a mystery over one of the entries.' She began talking faster so as to forestall any interruption. 'It's this line here. Can you make head or tail of it? Incidentally, I suppose it is your husband's writing?'

Diana glanced at the entry with seeming reluctance.

'I'm afraid I can't help you,' she said. 'I've no idea what it means. But it's my husband's writing.'

'Was he given to putting things in code?' Rosa enquired with a tentative smile.

'Why do you want to know these things and why should I talk to you about matters I'd sooner forget?'

'As you know, Mrs Wenning, my client was killed before a verdict was ever reached. He always denied having murdered Ching and I feel I owe it to him to clear up one or two unexplained details which may, or may not, cast light on his denial.'

'And what will be your reward at the end of it all?'

'I've not thought of it in terms of reward. It certainly won't be financial because the case is over and finished as far as the authorities are concerned. I suppose you could say that my reward will come in satisfying my curiosity. Incidentally, don't run away with the idea, Mrs Wenning, that I'm a sentimental female lawyer who thinks all her clients are blue-eyed angels. In point of fact, I believe that Kedby was blackmailing your husband, which was a deplorable thing to do. But it doesn't happen to be the offence with which he was charged.' She sat back and thrust away her hair which had fallen forward across both cheeks.

'You sound an unusual sort of solicitor,' Diana said with a faint smile. 'When did you qualify?'

'Only two years ago.'

'And you're already a partner!'

'Robin Snaith was a one-man band and I was originally his litigation clerk. Soon after I'd qualified he offered me a partnership.'

'In order to retain your services, no doubt,' Diana observed. She glanced down at the diary that lay on the table beneath them. 'My husband got up to quite a lot of things about which he wouldn't have wished me to find out,' she went on in a musing tone. 'It certainly wouldn't surprise me to learn that he employed his own private code in case I, or anybody else, happened to see something we shouldn't. However, as I said, I can't help you at all over this particular entry. Why don't you speak to my son-in-law about it? He, it seems, knew rather more about my husband's outside interests than I did.' Noticing Rosa's slightly startled expression she added, 'He raised loans to help my husband pay his gambling debts and things of that sort.' Her tone was bitter. Then glancing at her watch she said, 'If you're not in any hurry, stay and have a cup of coffee. I usually have one around now.'

'Thank you, I'd like to.'

Like many people left alone in a strange room, Rosa gravitated towards the bookshelf. She had spotted a leather-bound copy of the collected short stories of de Maupassant and wondered whether it was the same edition as she possessed. She took it from the shelf and opened it. There was an inscription on the first page which read: *D.W. happy birthday and love, G.W. May 1965.*

Though she regarded it as a perfectly acceptable

birthday present, the inscription struck her as curiously stilted, coming from one spouse to the other. She had just returned the book to the shelf when Diana Wenning returned with the coffee.

'I'm afraid I can never resist taking a look at people's books,' Rosa said, half-apologetically.

'They're meant to tell you more about their owner than anything else, I believe,' Diana remarked drily. 'I had to get rid of several hundred when I moved here. There just isn't the space. But I couldn't part with my Maupassant stories.'

Rosa had the clear impression that it was the book and not its donor that mattered.

While they had their coffee, Diana Wenning plied Rosa with questions about her work, though studiously avoiding any further reference to her husband or to the case that had brought Rosa to her front door. It seemed to her that Judge Wenning's widow had retired behind so many protective veils that it was impossible to know what contact, if any, one was making with the real person.

It was with a distinct feeling of relief that Rosa thanked her and said goodbye.

'I'm afraid Mr Snaith is out,' Stephanie, their Girl Friday, said when Rosa called the office.

'It doesn't matter, Stephanie, I have one further visit I want to make and then I'll be in.' She glanced at her watch. 'Should be in about a couple of hours' time.'

Although she supposed that, strictly speaking, she was no longer Arthur's solicitor, she couldn't regard her legal obligation towards him as terminated by his death. Somebody would have to attend to his funeral arrangements and if she didn't, who would? He had told her that he didn't have any relatives he was aware of.

On one of her prison visits he had given her a key to his flat for safe-keeping and it was there she decided she ought to go. Though he had never mentioned a will (there had been no reason to do so) she felt she ought to make a search of his drawers to see if there was one hidden away.

As she got out of the taxi outside his building, a woman, dragging a screaming child behind her, came up the steps from the basement flat. The woman was taking no notice of the child and was hauling it up the steps like an unwieldy sack. Rosa gave her a glance and wondered if she knew the recent gruesome history of where she was now living.

Arthur Kedby's room had a stale, sour, unoccupied smell and she somehow felt much more of an intruder than she had on the two occasions she had called to collect items to take him in prison.

All his papers appeared to be stuffed into a single drawer and she pulled it right out and carried it over to the table to sort through its contents.

But there was no sign of a will, or of anything which offered a clue to the personal wishes of its late occupant. She found a standard tenancy agreement and a bank statement showing a credit balance of £176 on the 4th October last. There was also a further bank statement showing £600 in a deposit account. If he had been successfully blackmailing Judge Wenning, it wasn't reflected in his bank account.

All the time she worked through the jumble of paper, half her mind continued to worry at the entry in the judge's diary.

Suddenly she sat bolt upright and stared straight ahead with an expression of furious concentration. It was the inscription in the Maupassant book that had floated into her mind with cathartic effect. Reaching excitedly into her bag for the diary, she opened it at the page that haunted her thoughts.

For several seconds she stared at it, her lips silently moving as though repeating an incantation.

She wondered if she could be right and, more important, how she was going to persuade anybody that her interpretation made sense and wasn't wild speculation. She would have to find outside proof to back up her hunch and at the moment hadn't the remotest idea where she could obtain it.

Nevertheless, she felt an upsurge of exhilaration and although deflation would surely follow unless she could substantiate her theory, she had never been unduly daunted by difficulties.

On arriving at her office, she found that Robin had been back, but had gone out again and that Douglas Orden had been calling her.

'He phoned a second time,' Stephanie said, 'even though I told him on the first occasion that you wouldn't be back until now.' She glanced at the temporarily un-manned switchboard which had blinked into sudden life. 'That could be him.' She hurried across and plugged herself in. A second later she gave Rosa a nod, accompanied by thumbs up sign.

Rosa went to her office and lifted the receiver.

'Rosa Epton speaking.'

'This is Douglas Orden, Miss Epton. I understand you visited my mother-in-law this morning and she seems to think I may be able to help you over an entry in Judge Wenning's diary.'

'I'd be very glad if you could, Mr Orden.'

'I'll be driving down to the Cotswolds later this afternoon, but I could drop in at your office within the next hour, if that's convenient.'

'I'll be here and shall look forward to seeing you.'

Forty minutes later he arrived. As soon as he was shown into her office, she recalled having seen him at court.

'We seem to have been among yesterday's lucky ones,' he said as they shook hands. 'I know you by sight, of course, Miss Epton, as I was sitting at the back of the court.' He pulled out a packet of cigarettes. 'Do you smoke?' Rosa shook her head. 'Mind if I do?' After he had lit up, he glanced round the room with a faintly glowering expression. His moustache seemed to give him a surly look. Returning his gaze to her, he said, 'I'm afraid my father-in-law has left quite a trail of destruction behind him. As you can imagine, it's been a traumatic experience for his family, though my mother-in-law has weathered the storm with remarkable resilience. More than my wife has, I'm afraid.' He again glanced at Rosa as if to assess her reaction. But her expression was one of polite, though uncommitted interest. 'I suppose because he had no son of his own I was drawn increasingly into my father-in-law's confidence. The fact that I was almost closer to his age than to my wife's also helped. I must say, however, that it was a responsibility I could have done without at times, particularly when it came to coping with his gambling debts. I take it you know about them?'

'Yes,' Rosa said with a small nod.

'The worst part was keeping it all from my mother-in-law, who didn't have an inkling of what he was up to. As a matter of fact, I didn't even dare tell my wife the whole story. There were times, Miss Epton, when I didn't know what to do next. There he was, a respected judge with a private life collapsing about his ears and me the only person aware of what was happening.'

It seemed to Rosa that he was going to great trouble to win her confidence and she wondered why.

'Do I gather from what you've just said,' she asked, 'that Judge Wenning told you he was being blackmailed by Ching?'

Her question seemed to halt him in his tracks, for he blinked and frowned for several seconds before answering. 'No, that was something he kept to himself. Understandably, I think. He wouldn't have wanted anyone to know about that particular caper. Gambling debts are one thing, but chasing after male prostitutes and being blackmailed is rather different. As we know, the poor man was finally driven to suicide by the secret shame of it all.'

'I came to regard Judge Wenning as a Hamlet figure who remained firmly in the wings,' Rosa remarked.

He nodded and glanced rather obviously at his watch. 'I'd like to get away before the evening traffic builds up...' he murmured.

'Of course.' Rosa reached into a drawer of her desk for the diary. Handing it to him, she said, 'That's the entry I can't make any sense of.'

Putting on a pair of heavy horn-rimmed spectacles which emphasised his lowering expression, he stared hard at the page at which she had opened it. He thrust out his lips with an air of judicial consideration. Then looking up, he said, 'I'm sorry, Miss Epton, but I can't help you. I've no idea what the entry means.'

He flicked idly through a few more pages before closing the diary and placing it on the edge of the desk.

'Oh, well, it was still good of you to get in touch and come along. I'm sorry it's proved to be a wasted journey.' As she finished speaking, she got up abruptly. 'Will you excuse me a moment? I must catch my partner before he goes out again.' Before he could say anything, she had disappeared from the room. When she returned three minutes later, she said a trifle breathlessly, 'I apologise for leaving you like that.'

'That's quite all right,' he said heartily. 'As a matter of fact, I must be on my way now.' He jumped up from his chair and Rosa accompanied him to the door. 'Don't bother to see me out, Miss Epton, I can find my own way.'

Rosa watched him stride quickly down the passage towards the main door. Finding it locked, he swung round and stared at her with a puzzled frown. At the same moment, Robin Snaith emerged into the corridor from his office.

'The door seems to be locked and I'm in a bit of a hurry,' he said to Robin.

'I think you're taking away something that doesn't belong to you, Mr Orden,' Rosa said as she advanced towards him.

'Is this some sort of a joke?' he asked angrily.

'I'd like the diary back,' Rosa said.

'What are you talking about?'

'The diary you took from my desk while I was out of the room.'

'It's probably on the floor. Have you looked under your desk? And now I must go, so kindly unlock the door.'

'It's not on the floor, because I've looked,' Rosa said. 'Why don't you feel in your pocket? I've an idea you'll find it there.'

'You're trying to trap me,' he said furiously.

'You seem to forget that it was your suggestion you should come and look at that entry in the diary. And very keen you were to do so, too!'

'And very sorry now that I ever offered to help you.'

'I suspect you weren't entirely motivated by kindness. Are you going to return it or must I phone the police?'

He stared at her incredulously. 'What the hell have the police got to do with it?'

'Because you're guilty of stealing.'

'I can sue you for that,' he said in a tone into which fear had crept. 'In any event, it's not your property, it's part of my father-in-law's effects.'

'It's an official court exhibit,' Rosa retorted, hoping that he wouldn't try and argue the niceties of legal owner-ship. 'Are you going to return it or not?'

For several seconds he stood in apparent indecision. Then putting his hand into his jacket pocket he brought out the diary and tossed it to Rosa.

'I don't know what all the fuss is about,' he said with a sneer.

'I suspect you know only too well. I believe you immediately realised what a damaging entry that was. So damaging to you that you determined to get hold of the diary so that you could destroy it. My only trap was to leave the room and give you the opportunity of taking it. I'd have been more than surprised if I'd returned and discovered you hadn't pocketed it. You see, Mr Orden, I'm pretty sure I know the significance of $2\frac{1}{2}$gdoret.'

Before she could say anything more, he had pushed Robin violently aside and had disappeared through the fire door and down the emergency stairs.

'Now perhaps you'd tell me what that was all about,' Robin said when he had recovered from his surprise.

'In a minute, Robin. But first I must call Chief Inspector Pennerly and tell him who murdered Ching.'

CHAPTER 24

A few days later, George Young entered the smoking room of Noone's Club and gazed round for somebody to talk to. The fact that he made a point of knowing every member by name didn't mean that he necessarily enjoyed all their company.

Spotting a face he had not seen for some time, he walked over to where the person was sitting.

'Not seen you in here for a long while,' he said over the top of the paper the man was reading. 'Hope you've not been ill.'

'I've been in South Africa for six months. Only got back yesterday morning.'

'Missed all our rotten weather, you lucky chap!'

'That was the whole idea.'

'I suppose you've not heard about the club's *cause célèbre*. More of a scandal actually.'

'What was that?'

'Remember that chap Kedby? The one you thought was in the secret service? Nothing of the kind. He was a common blackmailer who later turned to murder.'

'Good lord! I remember it was you who told me his name. Has he been found guilty?'

'The trial ended abruptly last week when some madman threw a grenade in court and killed Kedby. Didn't mean to kill him, I gather. Got the wrong person in the wrong court.'

'I remember reading something about it in a paper a day or so before I left Cape Town. It didn't mention any names, however.'

'Probably the kindest thing that could have happened to him.'

'Unless, of course, he happened to be innocent.'

'He'd never have been charged unless the police were certain he'd done it.'

'I used to believe that if the police charged somebody they must be guilty, but I'm less sure now.'

'He was guilty all right. As far as I can gather, he's the first member of the club ever to have stood trial for murder. Not a particularly meritorious record to have broken, eh!'

With this final comment, George Young strolled off in search of further prey.

At about the same time Arthur Kedby's name was being traduced in Noone's Club, Rosa and Greg were watching his mortal remains slide from their sight in the crematorium chapel. Shortly afterwards the brief service came to an end and they made their way outside.

'It's the first time I've been to a cremation,' Greg said with a shiver. 'Will his body be in the oven already?'

'Probably. They don't store them up until the end of the day.'

'I suppose not.' He glanced up at the crematorium chimney and shivered again. 'I don't think I want to be cremated.'

'Was your friend Tony buried?'

'His body was flown back to Hong Kong. It took his family a couple of weeks to raise the money and it must have cost them a bomb.' He paused as another funeral cortège, consisting of over half a dozen cars, drew up outside the chapel. 'Poor old Arthur had only you and me to see him off. It's a shame more people didn't know about his funeral.'

Rosa doubted whether there would have been any more mourners, even if the news had been broadcast by the B.B.C. She refrained, however, from saying so.

She had come in her car and offered Greg a lift back into central London. She dropped him at Hammersmith Broadway and watched him disappear into the crowd, a sad and lonely figure who was probably destined to remain so for the rest of his life.

When she got back to her office, Stephanie told her that Pennerly had been on the phone. He hadn't left any message, other than to ask that she should ring him back when she had a free moment.

She had heard nothing from him since her phone call following Douglas Orden's abrupt departure down the fire escape. He had sent a young officer round at once to pick up the diary, but, thereafter, had come silence.

She went to her office and put through a call to his station.

'I gather you were at Kedby's funeral when I rang,' he said.

'Yes. I was fifty per cent of the congregation.'

'Who was the other fifty per cent?' he asked in an interested voice.

'Greg.'

'Good for him! As you know, at one time I suspected him of having murdered Ching. Mind you, he was a fairly obvious suspect. Much more so than Kedby.'

'Who was also innocent.'

'Of murder, yes.' After a pause he went on, 'I was calling to give you a progress report. It seemed the least I could do in view of your help.'

'You mean you're satisfied that Orden did it?'

'Yes, though proving it may take a bit of work. We've

interviewed him a number of times and I get the impression that he hasn't enjoyed the experience. He's being very evasive, but, with luck, we'll catch him out in a few lies.

'I don't know if he didn't trust his wife to say he was home on the evening in question, but he went out of his way to give us an elaborate alibi for the night Ching was killed. Said he was in London on business and spent the evening with a certain Percy Sugarman, whom we know as a bit of a villain. We've been in touch with Sugarman who's in Spain at the moment and not surprisingly he supported Orden's story. As luck will have it, however, we happen to know that Sugarman and his brother were in Chester that evening. A small matter of observation by the lads at the Yard who take an interest in the movement of stolen antiques. We told Orden that Sugarman didn't support his alibi, which wasn't exactly the truth, and he immediately began hinting that one of them had murdered Ching on a contract put out by his father-in-law . . . So you can see he's got himself into something of a tangle. If we can trace the two and a half thousand pounds to him, that'll be a big help, but it appears to have been paid over in cash. It went into Wenning's account and was drawn out almost immediately by a cash cheque. I've no doubt that when Wenning agonised with his son-in-law what to do about Ching, Orden offered to get rid of him for cash on the nail. It must have seemed like fairly easy money.'

'Where did Judge Wenning raise that sort of money? He was usually borrowing from Orden, not paying him large sums.'

'I know. He borrowed this particular amount from a local businessman whom he had met at a function in Uxbridge and whose son was due to come up at West Middlesex Crown Court on a charge of robbery.'

'Do you mean he accepted a bribe?'

'The businessman, as you would expect, denies any such

interpretation. Says it was a friendly loan. As for his son, he later appeared before another judge and was given a two-year suspended sentence. So you can make what you like of it.'

'Has Orden admitted he knew what $2\frac{1}{2}$gdoret meant?'

'No. Says it's far-fetched guesswork on everyone's part.'

'I wish you could have seen his face when I told him that I knew,' Rosa said.

'I'd like to have been there,' Pennerly said with relish. 'But you'll be able to describe it to the court when we eventually get him there.' Then, as if savouring each syllable, he murmured, 'Two and a half grand Douglas Orden re Tony. Simple and crude, but quite ingenious. And very bright of you, Miss Epton, to decypher it. I must remember to call you up next time I'm stuck on an anagram in my crossword.'

Knowing Chief Inspector Pennerly as a tenacious and persevering officer, Rosa had no doubt that it would be only a matter of time before Douglas Orden was charged with Tony Ching's murder.

And this time it would be the right person.